DEATH-CHASE

The Lincoln was picking up speed and Frost cut the wheel of the Cadillac hard right, easing up on the gas, paralleling the car slightly ahead of it. The subgunner was firing point blank at Frost in the Cadillac now, the Cadillac's windshield spiderwebbing under the impact of the full metal case subgun ammo, the thudding against the body panels maddening.

Frost stuck the muzzle of the Metalifed High Power out the open window, over the jagged knife edges of glass, his left fist balled hard around the grips as he pumped the trigger toward the rifleman.

One shot, two, then two more and the slide locked open. The rifle discharged, the barrel swinging upward and a tongue of orange flame visible from the muzzle for an instant. Frost tossed his pistol onto the seat beside him, the subgunner opening up again. Frost wrenched the steering wheel hard left, then stomped the gas pedal, throwing himself across the seat as the Cadillac broadsided the Lincoln.

He could feel his body shake, his breath short, almost robbed from him as the impact came. There was a crunching of metal, a groaning, and Frost looked down—part of the firewall on the driver's side had buckled and had he stayed behind the wheel he would have lost his legs.

#12

THEY CALL ME

THE MERCENARY

HEADSHOT!

BY AXEL KILGORE

ZEBRA BOOKS
KENSINGTON PUBLISHING CORP.

For Sergeant Larry Allen, the man with the judo belt, the gleaming dome, and the joke books, from Lindblom back in the sixties in Chicago.

ZEBRA BOOKS

are published by

KENSINGTON PUBLISHING CORP.
475 Park Avenue South
New York, N.Y. 10016

Printed in the United States of America

Chapter One

Frost sat in the car and waited. The girl he had never met, Oriana Vasquez, who desperately needed a bodyguard for her father, one of the top leaders of the anti-Castro underground, Omega Seven, was late. Frost glanced at the black faced Rolex Sea-Dweller on his left wrist. She was very late.

. Frost stepped out of the car, nervous, slamming the door of the rented LTD behind him as he walked the few yards toward where the beach began. It was hard to feel anything but naked in the Keys north of Big Pine Key and south of Marathon. Ahead of him toward the Florida Peninsula, below Marathon, was little else but water and the ribbon of highway — the Overseas Highway — which connected the freckles of land like a dot-to-dot puzzle.

He looked around — there was no one in sight. The one-eyed man stripped away the jacket of his rumpled white suit and walked back toward the Ford, tossing the jacket onto the front seat after first retrieving his half-empty pack of Camels and the battered Zippo windlighter. He lit a cigarette, putting the rest of the pack in the breast pocket of his shirt, dropping the lighter in his left side trouser pocket. He hauled the black silk crocheted tie farther down from the open collar of his white shirt, well below half mast. "Shit," he murmured, glancing at the watch again.

Feeling conspicuous, despite the fact no one was in sight, he slipped out of the Cobra Gunskin Comvest. Before tossing the shoulder holster on the front seat, he ripped the Metalifed High Power from the leather, opened the front lower button of his shirt and stuffed the gun inside across his abdomen. It wasn't comfortable there, the black rubber Pachmayr grips sticking to his sweating skin, but it was better than being unarmed or appearing otherwise.

He pulled the little Gerber MkI boot knife, sheath and all, from where he carried it near the small of his back and dropped it in his right side pocket. "Damn," he murmured, glancing to his watch again.

Clandestine meetings of any kind made him nervous. He remembered the set-up in the Italian Alps with the defecting female terrorist and what had almost happened—his death.* There had been other secret meetings, with equally hair-raising results. He wasn't in the mood for it today.

And there was Bess to worry about, slightly angry with him for not coming back to her, but instead going to help out his old friend Lew Wilson in Florida Department of Law Enforcement. Lew had told him that Oriana Vasquez's father insisted he needed a bodyguard, because there was a traitor in Omega Seven. Not even his daughter Oriana took the old man seriously, but a bodyguard needed to be hired. The police could have done it, but the old man didn't trust police that much either. Would Frost help out, just

*See, They Call Me The Mercenary #9, *The Terror Contract*

until someone could be found to replace him—as a favor? Frost wondered why he had agreed—to help his pal Lew or to avoid settling on whether or not he and Bess would marry now, now that Eva Chapmann was dead.* While Eva had been alive, stalking him, wanting his death more than anything else, both Frost and Bess had known that a life of their own was impossible. But now? Frost, despite his love for Bess, had a hard time picturing himself married.

The one-eyed man started walking back toward the beach. He glanced again at the Rolex. If Oriana Vasquez didn't arrive in ten more minutes, he would leave, drive to Miami and tell Lew, "Thanks, but no thanks. If the Vasquez dame couldn't keep the meeting, her father can find himself another boy."

Frost found himself verbalizing the thought. "Goin' bananas," he smiled. The cigarette was burning his fingertips and he dropped it to the sand, heeling it out under his sixty-five dollar shoes.

Frost lit another cigarette, clicking the cowling of the Zippo closed with a vengeance, then dropping the lighter back in his pocket. He glanced at the watch again. "Five more lousy minutes—all you got, lady, then kiss off," and he kept walking. The sea was tranquil-seeming, little motion at all, the air still, no breeze stirring it for the moment.

Out beyond the periphery of land now, on a rough tangent to the line of the highway on the Atlantic side, he could see a small power boat. It was sitting dead in the water, a man apparently fishing from it.

*See, They Call Me The Mercenary #11, *Deathlust*

The boat made Frost nervous as well.

"The hell with it," the one-eyed man rasped, turning on his heel and starting back toward the rented Ford.

He froze in his tracks, the sound coming up from the Florida Bay side familiar—potentially deadly.

"Helicopter—damnit," he snarled, starting to run, reaching under his shirt and snatching at the Pachmayr gripped Browning, jerking back the hammer to full stand, the car now less than fifty yards from him, the helicopter—a bubble-domed Bell—making a low pass.

Frost hit the sand less than ten yards from the car, rolling behind the trunk of a gnarled palm, the sand erupting in tiny explosions as submachinegun fire rained down in a ragged line from the chopper. Frost fired the Browning once, twice, then twice more, the 115-grain JHPs slamming audibly against the skeletonized tail section of the helicopter, audibly and uselessly, he thought. The chopper finished the pass and Frost pulled himself to his feet. He heard another engine noise and as he reached the trunk of the LTD he looked around. The small motor launch was coming landward, in a hurry. "Hell!" Frost snarled, fumbling the trunk key, popping the trunk and reaching into his Safariland SWAT bag. He tore open the zippers, grabbing for the new, KG-99 9mm assault pistol. The successor to the original KG-9, it fired from a closed bolt, had a vertical front pistol grip and flash deflector. Now Frost rammed a thirty-six round magazine in place and worked the bolt.

The helicopter was making another pass, the subgunner leaning out of the bubble dome, firing.

Frost grabbed two spare sticks for the KG-99 and jumped, rolling down a small embankment, the sand around him chewing up under the impact of the sub-gun fire, the sound of bullets ricochetting off the rented Ford whistling from behind him.

On his back, palm trees on either side of him, his sixty-five dollar shoes filled with sand and the helicopter circling for another pass, Frost levelled the KG-99. The gun bucked in his hands, a two-shot semi-automatic burst going toward the bubble dome itself.

Frost could hear shouting. "Hank—hold on!"

Frost wheeled, on his knees, aiming at the bubble of the chopper, shifting the muzzle of the KG-99 quickly toward his shot-up car. Just as he was about to fire, he saw the face belonging to the voice. Large framed glasses dominated it, and the neatly trimmed dark hair tumbled across the forehead above them as the man ran. The chin, always a little deliberate, was jutted out. And in the man's right hand was an almost black-looking automatic pistol, in the left hand a smaller pistol, shiny, the muzzle gapingly large. "Hold on, Hank!"

"Lew!"

Frost heard the shout coming from his throat, felt the corners of his downturned mouth raise into a smile, then swept the muzzle skyward, the KG-99 belching fire, gunfire coming from Wilson's position as well now.

The helicopter shot hard right, over a rise of ground and seaward. Frost pushed himself to his feet, running back up the embankment. Lew Wilson was already crouched beside the rented LTD, the big black autoloader in his right fist pumping across the

9

front passenger door.

"They're makin' another pass, Hank!" Wilson shouted.

Frost hit the road and dove toward the car, beside Wilson. "Hi, Lew—what's cookin'?"

"Aww, shut up," Wilson laughed.

Frost pushed himself to his feet, running around the passenger side door, flipping up onto the hood of the LTD and rolling across, the metal burning hot to his bare hands from the sun. Frost rolled off the driver's side of the hood, snatching open the driver's side door, ducking behind it as the helicopter started in.

Wilson wasn't shooting and Frost looked through the driver's seat. Wilson was changing sticks. "Beretta?"

"Yeah—92SB," Wilson answered, ramming the fresh magazine up the well and turning back toward the helicopter.

Frost dumped the magazine from the KG-99 and rammed a fresh one home, waiting.

The subgunner in the bubble dome was opening up. Frost started to fire, and from his right across the driver's seat by the open opposite door he could hear Wilson firing again.

Frost raised the assault pistol up, firing rapid, two-shot semi-automatic bursts. With the third burst Frost thought he might have hit the bubble. The helicopter seemed to hesitate in mid-air, almost imperceptibly. The chopper elevated rapidly, Frost looking up.

"Holy shit! Lew—grenades!" Frost grabbed his coat and shoulder rig from the seat and pushed himself away from the LTD, ducking his head into the still-open trunk and grabbing out his SWAT bag as he did, then diving over the embankment, toward the beach side.

The concussion made his already ringing ears feel as if they'd explode, burning pieces of hot metal and fabric raining down on him as Frost burrowed into the sand.

The one-eyed man felt the pelting against his body stop, heard the roaring again of the rotor blades overhead, but the sound dull because of his ears, like hearing a wave in a conch shell. He rolled onto his back, the helicopter above him. He could see Lew Wilson, standing now by the side of the road, the Beretta 92SB pumping lead upward at the chopper. Frost, from flat on his back, started firing the KG-99. There was a man leaning from the chopper, something small and dark in his right fist.

Frost emptied the KG-99's magazine at him and scrambled to his feet.

The sound and the rush of air slapped at him—it was the only explanation Frost could think of as he hit the sand, rolling. He squinted against the debris that filled the air. The chopper—a fireball, orange and black and rising on a heat thermal was belching skyward, chunks of helicopter and pieces of human bodies crashing downward.

The one-eyed man pushed himself to his feet, the KG-99 slung across his right shoulder, muzzle downward.

Lew Wilson had shoved his pistol into his belt and was cleaning his glasses. As Wilson started across the scorched roadside, past the still-burning hulk of the Ford, Frost could barely hear Wilson over the ringing in his ears. But he thought Wilson was saying, "Glad

11

to see you haven't changed any, Hank."

Frost smiled and shrugged, then started searching his pockets for a cigarette. Things rarely changed at all.

Chapter Two

"Naw—I don't think Oriana Vasquez had a thing to do with it—really Hank."

Frost eyed Lew Wilson beside him at the bar. "Then why didn't she show up?"

"Probably got tipped something might be going down—I don't know."

Frost lit a Camel in the blue-yellow flame of his battered Zippo. "Then why didn't she contact your office?"

"I told you—she doesn't like cops."

"Nuts—change the subject. When you switch to a Beretta 92?"

"92SB," Wilson noted. "With the magazine release up by the trigger guard. Hell of a good gun. Fifteen-round magazine."

"And that mini-cannon—a Detonics .45?"

"Back up gun—really like it. You got one of those new KG-99s, huh?"

"Yeah," Frost answered, sipping at his rum and Coke. "My buddy at Interdynamics makes a good gun—feeds hollow points as well as my Browning, right out of the box. With loaded mags in each gun, I've got forty-nine rounds I can spit without reloading. Nice firepower."

"You ready to talk about what you wanted to talk about, or you want to talk guns some more?"

"Shut up, Lew," Frost laughed. Wilson clapped him on the shoulder and Frost turned around. The hostess was signalling to them.

"Come on—bring your drink." Wilson left the bar and started across into the dining room, Frost following him. It had been a long time since he'd seen his old friend—not since the poop he'd gotten on drug smuggling out of Asia that had taken him—Frost—to Burma and the Golden Triangle.*

The hostess set two menus down on a table beside a massive plate glass window, Wilson already seating himself, Frost starting to sit down across from him. Beyond the window was a boat dock, and beyond the dock the comparatively calm waters of a small harbor. Sailcraft and motorized pleasure boats were either wharfed or going in or out through the harbor mouth, and seagulls, offwhite in color and gliding in controlled frenzy, zig-zagged over the few persons walking back and forth along the docks.

"I'm glad we're eating inside," Frost observed. "Those things'll snatch food right out of your hand."

"Yeah, they're everywhere, too. So," and Wilson looked down into his hands, as if studying them. "What you been doin'?"

"Stuff I shouldn't tell a cop about, probably—I tracked down a woman who was trying to kill me.

*See, The Call Me The Mercenary #4, *The Opium Hunter*

14

Long story.* Not a very pretty one. But that's behind me now."

"How about you and Bess—or shouldn't I ask?"

"You can ask whatever you want. Hell—if I knew what to tell you, I might know what to tell myself," and Frost laughed, downing his rum and Coke and lighting another cigarette while he studied the menu. Everything was expensive, but Frost didn't care—Wilson was treating. He decided on a combination of snow crab legs and steak, then looked up from the menu. "So—you think Oriana Vasquez was on the level?"

"As much as she ever is—gee, I really love the way you pick up conversations from—"

"How you like that Detonics .45?"

"Aww, go to—"

Frost laughed, holding up his right hand, palm outward, in a mock gesture of surrender. "Okay—tell me about it."

"Not a lot to tell, really," Wilson began. He started to speak, then stopped, the waitress coming, Frost ordering, then Wilson ordering the same. They each ordered drinks again, Frost re-specifying Myers dark rum with his rum and Coke.

Frost lit a cigarette, staring out the window at the seagulls and the water, waiting for Wilson to begin again once the waitress took the menus. After a moment, Wilson said, "You know about Omega Seven—the anti-Castro underground in and around Miami. And you know Colombia's M-19 terrorists.

*See, They Call Me The Mercenary #10, *Bush Warfare;* They Call Me The Mercenary #11, *Deathlust.*

15

And you know about the drug traffic—marijuana and cocaine, some pills, stuff like that. So, put 'em all together into a card shuffler and whataya got?"

Frost looked at Wilson. "A lot of killing?"

"That's what you got. See, a lot of the drug smuggling is being done by pro-Castro Cubans and a lot of Colombians. A lot of the stuff originates in Colombia. Some of the stuff might be smuggled in from Communist Asian nations. I don't know. Lot of screwy stuff. But anyway, a while back some of the drug smugglers started working hand in hand with M-19—and it got scary real quick."

"What do you mean?" Frost asked through a cloud of exhaled cigarette smoke.

"I mean, to get protection from the Colombian authorities—who are on our side fighting the drug smuggling, well, some of the smugglers started doing errands for M-19. Smuggling in stuff from Cuba that M-19 needed, smuggling explosives up from Colombia to pro-Castro terrorists here in Miami, arming them. Gone are the days of deadheading."

"But—"

"See," Wilson went on, sighing hard, staring down into his hands again, then looking up into Frost's face. "See, what apparently the pro-Castro people want to do is make it hot for the anti-Castro people, with the Cuban population and with the law. There was a plot a while ago back to use some of the Colombian explosives to blow up a senior citizen's cultural center, all Cubans there, then blame it on Omega Seven. We got wind of it, stopped it, but it was a near thing. Could have had sixty-eight people dead, more than a dozen of 'em in wheelchairs, as well as the people who

16

worked there. Also there was a nursery school next door with forty-three pre-school kids in it. No tellin' how much explosives they were gonna use—coulda blotted out those kids too."

"Wonderful," Frost observed, lighting another cigarette, Wilson waiting as the waitress brought the fresh drinks. "But you got the guys?" Frost finally asked.

"No—got one guy, shot up when we tried nailing him. We learned he was the bomb delivery man, but no bomb. Hadn't picked it up yet, and he died before we could get him to a hospital."

"Rats."

"Exactly—so all that explosives, all the rest of the stuff they've brought in since, all still sittin' out there. Just waiting. Now—add to that—"

"Wait," Frost interrupted. "What do you need me for—sounds like police business pure and simple."

"It is—but with one little hitch: Oriana Vasquez's father. See, he doesn't trust cops, but he still wants to work within the law. His daughter doesn't care one way or the other. So it's to everyone's advantage that Señor Vasquez stays alive, doing what he's doing. Now, he is convinced there's a traitor in Omega Seven, someone highly placed who has tight connections to the Castro people. His daughter doesn't think so, and it looks like there probably isn't a traitor—just good solid intelligence work on the part of the pro-Castro people. But there have been two attempts on Señor Vasquez's life. His wife, Oriana's stepmother, was killed in the first attempt. Señor Vasquez wanted a bodyguard from outside Omega Seven and ordered Oriana to come to us and see if we could recommend someone reliable."

"So, Vasquez doesn't trust the law, but he trusts the law enough to get help in finding a bodyguard. And the Castro people decided to knock me off before I took the job."

"Yeah, I know—sounds complicated, stupid," Wilson agreed. "But, when she came to us, I couldn't think of a better guy than you. That's why I contacted Diablo Security and that stiff up there—"

"Andy Deacon," Frost smiled.

"Yeah—well, he told me you were somewhere in the Mediterranean. Didn't take too long to track you down and get you the word."

"I can't work as the guy's bodyguard—I got other things—"

"I figured you'd say that," Wilson nodded. "But I figured I could connive you into taking it on for a couple of weeks until you or I could find somebody just as good to replace you."

"We could never find anybody just as good as me," Frost laughed.

Wilson nodded, smiling. "Well—I'm not gonna walk into that, but you know what I mean. I need somebody who can't be bought off or scared off, is too tough to kill and works well with a gun just in case there's another attempt on Señor Vasquez's life. If he dies before we track down those Colombian explosives, there's gonna be a bloodbath in all of south Florida. I guarantee it. His daughter'll go for it, all the way, and the pro-Castro people'll do the same."

"So, if I don't take the job, I could cause the deaths of a lot of innocent people?"

"You got it," Wilson said.

"You think that bothers a tough guy like me?"

"Yeah," Wilson said.

Frost shook his head, stubbing out his cigarette and looking across the table into Wilson's face. "You know—I hate people that are right."

Chapter Three

She was exquisite, but Latin women frequently could be that—exquisite, Frost thought. He studied her face across the flickering blue yellow flame of his battered Zippo as he lit a cigarette, then inhaled the smoke deep into his lungs. The cheekbones were high, the nose sculpted, it seemed—patrician looking; and the eyes were wide-set under long, dark lashes, the color a brilliant blue.

"So, you are Señor Frost—at last we meet," she smiled, extending her right hand. Frost took it in his—the handshake was firm, dry, warm. "Had I known that any act of violence was planned against you personally down there in the Keys. I would most certainly have contacted the authorities."

"Probably heard I was going to work for you— figured to get me out of the way. That kind of thing can happen."

"But your friend, Señor Wilson—he said there was not enough left of the bodies of the men in the helicopter to make any sort of identification. That is a pity."

"Probably a couple of Castro hit men," Frost nodded. "More where they came from." Frost gestured toward the car parked by the roadside in the city park. "We going for a ride?"

"Yes—to meet my father. He is the one, as you know, who insists on having a bodyguard outside our organization."

Frost gestured then toward the two men—big, beefy-looking, with obvious bulges under their coats—standing some twenty yards away, roughly equidistant between himself and the car. "They can't do the job?"

"It is not," she began, turning and starting to walk, "a lack of trust." Frost joined her, walking beside her into the park. She wore a blue and white floral print sundress, the thin straps that fought against gravity and held it up looking somehow lighter-colored than the dress itself against the deep tan of her shoulders. Walking beside her, he noticed too that she was tall for a woman, in the low-heeled shoes she wore perhaps five ten. "His distrust goes deeper than individuals. Those two—Juan and Alberto. He has known them since they were young boys."

"Big boys I bet," Frost interrupted.

As if he had said nothing, she went on. "But he feels there is someone within the organizational structure trying to kill him, perhaps for his own advancement, working with the Castro people. And that is why he wishes to hire you or a man like you—someone who could not possibly have anything to gain collaborating with the Communistas."

"What about you?"

She turned, staring at him, her eyes startled. "About me?"

"Yes—you really think this is all unnecessary?"

Her expression eased and she continued walking. "If my father feels the presence of a new bodyguard,

one from outside our organization, will be to his benefit, then I will go along with him. He needs the
rest—the mental fatigue is wearing at him."

Frost dropped his cigarette, heeling it out under his
shoe into the grass. "But you think he's dead
wrong—there is no traitor?"

"Si—there is no traitor."

"Then how did those jokers with the helicopter
know exactly where to find me and when? You knew,
Lew Wilson knew and I knew."

"You could have been seen at the airport, or at the
rental car agency, then followed. There are many
possibilities." She stopped walking, leaning against a
palm tree, a gentle wind blowing at her hair, a strong
gust for an instant ballooning the skirt of her sundress
up past her thighs.

Her legs were pretty, Frost thought.

"Why did you cancel out on the meeting—what
kind of information did you get that made you change
your mind?"

She licked her lips, looking away from him, then
into his eye. "I learned that there was perhaps a plot
afoot to kill me, and so I decided that if I were being
closely watched or followed, it would be senseless for
me to drive down that far into the Keys—you are
closer to Cuba there than to Miami. And obviously, I
would not be treated well in Cuba."

"Obviously," Frost agreed. He didn't like the vibes
he was getting. But it wasn't something definite and
he tried shaking it. "How did you learn there was a
plot against your life?"

"We have a well-developed intelligence system. Our
analysts interpreted bits and pieces of information

and—perhaps others would have drawn different conclusions. I was warned, and I obeyed the warning. It was obviously well that I did."

"Oh, yeah," Frost smiled. "You could have let me know."

"There was no time—and I did not think you would be in danger."

"Is that an apology?"

"If you wish it to be," she smiled. "And now—to meet my father?"

Frost nodded, following her as she turned on her heel and started abruptly back toward the car.

As he started into the car, he felt a hand on his shoulder. He looked around and up. The huge man behind him was smiling. Frost asked, "You Juan or Alberto?"

"Juan—and I must have your gun, Señor."

"No offense Juan—but piss on that."

Frost could see the big man's shoulders bunching, see the second man, Alberto, starting around from the front of the car.

"Wait!"

Frost took his eye off Juan for a moment, looking back into the car at Oriana. "She said to wait," Frost smiled back at Juan.

"It is all right for this man to go armed. My father will expect him to be so."

Frost glanced back at her, then at Juan. "You heard the lady. Any problems with it?"

Juan shook his head, looking something between embarrassed and disgusted, then stepped back to hold Frost's door. As Frost passed inside, he nodded, "Thanks, pal."

The drive was down the Florida coast and past Miami and after a time Frost turned to the girl. "How much longer—until we get to your father's place?"

"Another few minutes," she answered noncommittally, then turned away from him to continue staring out the window.

Frost shrugged and lit a cigarette, decided that the girl—Oriana—was singularly unfriendly. It was ten more minutes by the Rolex on his left wrist before the vehicle stopped in front of a modest home surrounded by a stone fence with an iron grillwork gate barring the driveway.

Juan, who had sat beside the driver, Alberto, climbed out and went to a speaker mounted beside the gate. Frost couldn't hear what the big man was saying, but the gates opened as Juan turned to re-enter the Cadillac. Alberto started the big car up the driveway, Frost looking through his side window. The one-eyed man could see more guards about the place—at least three—and assumed there were more he couldn't see. The three he'd spotted carried riot shotguns and wore full flap G.I. holsters for the .45s on their hips. One of the men, more slightly built than the rest, looked particularly bizarre, Frost thought. Riot shotgun and pistol belt, but all he wore were deck shoes and a pair of swimming trunks. Frost dismissed the oddity then—after all, he reasoned, it was Florida.

Gravel crunched audibly under the wheels as the car slowed, then stopped, less than a dozen yards from where three low steps rose from the driveway and led to a tunnel-like walkway leading toward double front doors.

Frost got out of the car, Oriana climbing out the other side as Alberto held her door.

Frost thought he caught something between Oriana and Alberto, but wasn't certain. But without crossing from the other side of the car, Oriana suddenly said, "I must go inside and find my father. You will wait here with Alberto and Juan. I shall only be a few minutes."

"Whatever," Frost shrugged, noticing a stone bench at the far side of the gravel driveway and gravitating toward it.

It was warm under the sun, and Frost watched as Alberto, then Juan after him, stripped away their coats and placed them inside the car. "Hot," Frost smiled.

Neither man answered.

Mechanically, Frost noted that Juan carried what appeared to be a .45 Government Model Colt, swathed in a standard right-side-up holster. But from what Frost could see, it appeared as though the grips the gun sported were ivory.

Alberto wore a double shoulder rig, both guns in a diagonal carry mode. From what Frost could see of the guns, they appeared to be Smith & Wesson Model 66s, the round butted snub-nosed variety.

"You guys are ready for anything, huh?" Frost smiled again.

Juan merely nodded. Frost heard gravel crunching behind him and stood up, turning around. It was the guy with the swimming trunks, the riot shotgun and the pistol belt, and behind him came two more men. Frost didn't like the looks in their eyes.

"Hey, guys—ahh—"

"I think you are a police spy," the one with the swimming trunks said.

"Si—this one knows the one named Wilson," Alberto added.

"We don't need a lousy damn spy here," another of the men standing beside the one with the swimming trunks added.

Frost looked at the latter speaker. He wore a tank top and walking shorts and had hair past shoulder length. "Maybe you don't need a spy, wise-ass, but you could use a barber," Frost smiled. "If you guys wanna pick a fight, I may as well have some fun too."

"A fight, huh," the one with the shorts smiled.

The one with the swimming trunks set down his riot shotgun, leaning it against the right rear fender of the Cadillac.

"Look guys," Frost smiled. "There're only five of you—I'd be taking unfair advantage."

Alberto laughed—too loudly, Frost thought.

Frost looked at him, smiling. "How about there's a company of Texas Rangers waiting to attack at my signal?"

Juan laughed.

"Texas Rangers are fierce fighters—I'm warning you suckers."

The one with the swimming trunks started to swing, a right haymaker and Frost dodged it, catching the man's right forearm against his own left. Then Frost's right arced up, tipping the man with the swimming trunks on the base of the jaw, hammering him back.

As Frost started to wheel, he felt something pound against his back, just missing his right kidney. Frost dropped to his knees, seeing Juan behind him, both fists still bunched together, the fists looking twice as large as two housebricks. His breath short from the blow to his back, Frost rammed his right fist out, straight-arming Juan in the crotch. The big man almost screamed, doubling over, his hands reaching out as Frost rolled back.

The one who needed the barber was coming and Frost scooped up a handful of dirt, hurtling it upward into the man's face, then rolled as Alberto jumped for him.

Frost was on his feet, but barely, as the last of the five men made his play. Frost feigned a savate kick with his right leg, then wheeled and back-kicked the man twice with his left foot, into the face, knocking him back. Frost spun around as Alberto came for him again. Alberto swung wildly with his left; Frost dodged under it, backslapping the knife edge of his left hand into Alberto's left rib cage, then wheeled, slamming his right elbow into Alberto's chest, then wheeled again, the heel of his right hand slamming upward under the base of Alberto's jaw.

Frost felt hands on his shoulders, backstepped and rammed his right elbow back, at the same time smashing down with his right foot onto the instep of his attacker's right foot.

Frost started to turn, but felt the hands that had been on his shoulders wrapping around his throat now. It had to be Juan, Frost reasoned. And now the one with the swimming trunks was coming at him too. Frost snapped his hands back, grabbing for Juan's face, ears, then falling back against the larger man, snapping his feet up into the chest of the man with the swimming trunks. There was a scream from behind him and the hands around Frost's neck loosened.

Frost half stumbled forward, wheeling, kicking the man with the swimming trunks in the side of the head, Juan charging at him like a wounded bull. Frost backstepped, rasping, "Take it easy, big guy—come on."

From Frost's right the one-eyed man could see the man who needed a barber, charging at him, fists flying in the air. Juan was racing toward him as well. Frost sidestepped right, snapping his left foot high, catching the one who needed a barber square in the chest.

Frost stepped back again. Juan, head low, was hurtling toward him. Frost feigned a kick, Juan sidestepping, then Frost came in from Juan's right, Frost's left fist hammering out and down, his knuckles taking the full impact as his fist crashed against the man's right cheekbone. Juan reeled, straightened himself and lunged. Frost sidestepped, wheeling, snapping a low kick into Juan's crotch, then pivoted again, chopping down across the back of Juan's neck with the knife edge of his right hand.

Juan staggered, dropped to his knees.

Frost backstepped one pace and started to swing a kick with his right foot at the big man's head.

"Enough!"

Juan dropped back on his haunches. Alberto, starting to his feet, leaned against the bench. The one wearing the swimming trunks smiled and stepped away.

Frost looked into the tunnel-like entrance to the house. A small white-haired man wearing glasses and a pointed white spade beard stood there.

"Capitan Frost—you are hired," the old man said with something sounding like a mixture of amusement and embarrassment.

Frost looked at the old man hard, still flexing his right fist, the knuckles stinging from hitting Juan in the cheekbone. Then Frost murmured, "If this is how you test out a bodyguard, I'd hate to hire on as your driver—you'd probably cut the brake lines and disable the steering."

Some sixth sense, Frost pegged it as that when he felt it—he wasn't going to like this job.

Chapter Four

Frost closed the small black book—he had run through all the names he could think of. Wrong numbers, disconnects, out of towns and no answers—but always the same result. After a week of sheer boredom guarding Moises Vasquez, Oriana's father, he had found no one to replace himself. He had even tried Andy Deacon at Diablo Protective Services. Deacon himself was away on a job and none of the other guys were around, only the girl who answered the telephone, the same one who'd given Frost's clothes away to charity once.

Frost had left at least a dozen messages, with wives, girlfriends and electronic answering machines. As yet, no one had called back.

Stuffing the address book inside a hollowed-out Rogchild Hiding Book he had acquired, he placed it inside a pocket of his suit bag and zipped it shut. "Shit," he murmured. The last thing he wanted was to continue bodyguarding Moises Vasquez from what he had rapidly decided was an imaginary traitor, despite the fact he liked Vasquez personally. If Omega Seven exuded one thing, Frost decided, it was loyalty.

Frost looked at his watch—a full twenty minutes remained before Vasquez was due to leave for his meeting that day and the weather was uncomfortably hot. Despite the air conditioning, Frost was sweating. He stripped away his shirt and his slacks and underpants and started for the bathroom.

He stepped into the shower and turned on the water, mixing it to where it was barely less than cold, then turning up the shower head, standing under it. He started to wash his hair, wondering to himself when he'd actually get to the point where disgust overruled courtesy and he'd tell Moises Vasquez that he was leaving, tired of guarding against shadows. Frost rinsed his hair, starting to soap his body. It was the third shower he'd taken that day, little else to do in daylight hours besides shower, read adventure novels and make phone calls to people who weren't there. "Damn," Frost rasped, letting the water stream over his body, rinsing the soap away. He turned the water straight cold, but felt little difference—there was little in Florida besides ice cubes in mixed drinks that was very cold at all.

Frost revised the idea, thinking back to Oriana Vasquez. He shook his head, angry. He had never been so self-centered as to assume that every woman he met had to fall into bed with him, but this woman didn't even speak to him. And that made Frost angry—angrier as he thought about it, watching the water running over his chest, noticing the ever-increasing amount of grey in the hairs there. "Aagh!" Oriana Vasquez made him angry, and Frost disliked being angry, because he equated angry reaction with stupidity.

Frost shut off the water, stepping out of the shower and beginning to towel himself dry. He smiled, thinking the maid who supplied the fresh towels had to think he had a cleanliness fetish.

Frost left the jeans and T-shirt on the bed where he'd dropped them, searching through his drawers and finding dark blue socks that matched and a pair of underpants. He took a light blue shirt from the closet along with his khaki-colored tropical suit. He dressed quickly, finding a midnight-blue silk crocheted tie and knotting it loosely around his neck.

Mechanically, he checked the Browning High Power, dumping the magazine, jacking back the slide and catching the chambered round in the palm of his right hand. He reinserted the round into the magazine, making the magazine full with thirteen again. He slapped the spine of the magazine against the palm of his hand, then rammed the magazine up the well, then snapped back the slide, letting it run forward. Slowly, carefully, Frost lowered the hammer on the chambered round. Though he sometimes carried cocked and locked, and realized it was probably a safer carry mode, standing hammers always gave him the jitters, so he opted for the hammer down carry. And like many professional gunmen, he sacrificed one extra round—in the case of the Browning a fourteenth—for the smoother feeding which chambering the top round out of the magazine provided, the cycling action edging the new top round slightly forward.

He slipped the gun into the Cobra Comvest and eased the holster across his shoulders, finding his knife and extra magazines and dropping the magazines into his jacket pockets, instantly ruining the cut of his suit, then sliding the Gerber knife in its holster into position near the small of his back. He put on his coat.

He snatched up the KG-99 and shoved it into the black fabric Safariland SWAT bag, first checking that the spare magazines were loaded, then zipped the bag shut.

He started toward the door, stopping when there was a knock. Frost glanced at his watch—he wasn't late yet. He set down the SWAT bag and opened the door.

It was Oriana.

"Come in," Frost smiled, mildly shocked.

"There is no time—there will be a slight change in plans. Since I was coming this way—I had forgotten my handbag—my father asked me to tell you."

"What's the slight change?" Frost asked her.

"It appears that not only our branch of Omega Seven is—how would you put it—"

"Nervous?"

"Si—but so are some of the others. For the conference we will have, it will be necessary to keep an armed presence to a bare minimum. Only weapons that can be concealed under your clothing will be permitted—none of the other guards are bringing their shotguns or other special weapons."

Frost noticed her eyeing the black bag on the floor beside him. "Okay—no special weapons, just like the other—guards," he nodded. He left the bag on the floor where he'd dropped it, and followed Oriana out into the hall—already thinking at the back of his mind that he'd regret leaving the assault pistol . . .

Frost felt jittery, so near the Keys again so soon after the abortive attempt on his life. The car stopped and Alberto looked back at him. Frost gave the big man a nod, looking to Moises Vasquez then, saying, "Señor Vasquez—if you'll wait inside a moment with Juan, Alberto and I will take a look around."

"Whatever you say, Capitan Frost," Vasquez nodded, smiling.

As Frost exited the car, he reflected that the one and only good feature of bodyguarding Moises Vasquez had been meeting the man himself, the quiet talks they had had in the evenings, occasionally over a chessboard at which Frost had constantly been overwhelmed. Vasquez had been a scientist and university professor before the rise to power of Fidel Castro, and had narrowly escaped the island with his life, his first wife, Oriana's mother, dying during the escape attempt, Oriana little more than an infant.

Frost slammed the car door closed behind him, surveying the open expanse of green and the palm stands beyond. He disliked the idea of the meeting being so much in the open, but it was at the insistence of the other Omega Seven elements, and Moises Vasquez had agreed despite Frost's protests.

Already, in the distance, Frost spotted a car. Another condition of the meeting had been one car each, with whatever personnel were needed. With one exception—Oriana. She had come alone in a little Fiat Turbo sportster, selected by all concerned to moderate the little but important meeting, selected because, of all the personnel in Omega Seven, she was the most universally trusted. Her father was a leader, her mother had been killed while fleeing Cuba and her stepmother had been killed as well. Her loyalty was above reproach.

Frost watched her getting from her car, the car

parked in the middle of the clearing. She wore a dark blue sundress and because of the wind perhaps, or perhaps just for appearance, she was gathering a shawl around bare shoulders. Her hair was up, and she looked even more beautiful that way. "Hell," Frost rasped to himself.

The one-eyed man studied the clearing and the palm stands beyond. He saw no evidence of anyone lying in wait. "Alberto!"

"Si, Hank?"

"Go take up a position over by those trees—don't watch the meeting, but watch the trees—first sign of anyone out there, blow the whistle and—"

"I do not have a whistle—I can fire my guns."

"Right," Frost smiled. "You know—gimme a signal and we'll haul everybody out of here. Right?"

"Si—right," and Alberto started to run across the open area, toward the treeline.

Still another car was coming up. As Frost understood it there should be four cars in all, five counting Oriana's. Frost started back toward the Cadillac and Moises Vasquez, opening the rear passenger door on the driver's side and leaning inside. Señor Vasquez was studying his notes, but looked up, smiling. "Si, Capitan Frost?"

"Sir, I think it's just about time for you to get out." And Frost looked over his shoulder, awkwardly—because of the eyepatch—turning to look across his right shoulder to see something to his left. The occupants of the car that had just arrived were getting out, and the other car that had just pulled onto the field was stopping.

"Certainly—perhaps that is the advantage of an

outdoor meeting, without tables, without chairs—it will be a fast meeting and notes will be useless." Frost stepped back as Moises Vasquez began to exit the car. Juan was sliding out too, his coat open and Frost knew why—he could see the bulge of the ornate .45 the man carried habitually. Moises Vasquez apparently noticed it as well. "Remember, gentlemen—this is a meeting of friends, good men united by a common cause. There is no self-interest here, just a desire for freedom. So we can all trust one another."

Frost lit a cigarette, the blue-yellow flame of his battered Zippo flickering in the breeze that was blowing strongly now across the field. "It's your job to trust, Senor Vasquez—our job to distrust. If everyone does their job, everything will be fine."

"A realist—that is why your game of chess needs improving, Hank," Vasquez smiled. "You cannot fight your opponent's men as though they were real—you cannot suspend the reality of the situation."

"But here," Frost smiled, rather proud of himself for turning an intellectual-sounding phrase, "if they take my king, we all lose."

Vasquez looked at him a moment, amusement in the old man's eyes. "I shall ponder that, Capitan Frost—I shall ponder that."

"Yes, sir," Frost smiled. It had made sense to him.

Vasquez started away from the car, Juan dogging his footsteps, Frost hanging back, watching as the fourth car pulled off the road and into the field. It would be Eduardo Ruiz and his guards, Ruiz the only one of the four who drove other than a black bullet-proofed Cadillac—a grey, bullet-proofed Lincoln Town Car.

The car was moving steadily and Frost turned away from watching it, watching instead Moises Vasquez as he approached his daughter, Oriana. As Oriana leaned up to embrace him, the shawl fell from her shoulders and she stepped away, stooping quickly to pick it up.

Frost didn't know whether he heard the sound first or saw the thing that happened to Moises Vasquez's head.

The skull exploded, filaments of red and grey bursting from it almost in slow motion, the body lurching forward. Above the noise of gunfire, now everywhere around Frost, was the sound of Oriana Vasquez, screaming.

Frost snatched the High Power from the Cobra Comvest under his suitcoat, jacking back the hammer, half-wheeling as he went into a crouch. The grey Lincoln Town Car was stopped, a long, slender muzzle poked out the rear passenger window. Frost shot toward it, submachinegun fire from the front seat of the Lincoln spraying the open field. Frost could see Juan running toward it, then see Juan going down, his .45 discharging uselessly into the ground as he dropped, the front of his shirt and suit jacket riddled with bullet holes. The subgunner was changing the direction of his fire now and Frost could see the muzzle of the sniper rifle swinging toward him as well. Over the gunfire and Oriana's screaming, he could hear the wrenching and groaning of power steering, the screeching of tires as the other limos started across the ground. The grey car was moving now too. Frost fired at it again, one round, then another, then another and another. The rifle belched fire and Frost heard the window of the Cadillac behind him shattering. He hit the ground, eyeing the window for an instant—the driver's side glass was spider-webbed but still held together somehow. Frost hauled himself to his feet, running toward the Cadillac as subgun fire hammered into the ground around him, bullets pinging loudly off the body armor plate of the Cadillac.

Frost hit the car and dropped, the rifle booming again, the round's point of impact lost to him. Frost reached up, wrenching open the driver's side door, then threw himself inside across the front seat.

He looked back, the keys still in the ignition. "Thank God," he murmured, sitting up, twisting the key, gunning the engine, his foot down to the floor on the accelerator. He popped the transmission into drive, releasing the emergency brake simultaneously, the Cadillac shooting ahead. The driver's side door slammed shut as Frost wrenched the wheel of the armor-plated Cadillac into a hard right, the response slow because of the added weight of the body armor.

He could see Alberto, running from the stand of palms, firing both snubby Model 66s as he ran, toward the grey Lincoln. The Lincoln was picking up speed, the submachinegun still firing as Frost cut a hard left, then crushed the accelerator under his foot.

He could intercept it.

The Lincoln was picking up speed and Frost cut the wheel of the Cadillac hard right, easing up on the gas, paralleling the car slightly ahead of it. The subgunner was firing point blank at Frost in the Cadillac now, the Cadillac's windshield spiderwebbing under the impact of the full metal case subgun ammo, the thudding against the body panels maddening. Frost's palms sweated. He looked left, the muzzle of the rifle stabbing out the rear window again. Frost punched the button for the automatic window beside him, the window going down only two thirds of the way, the spider-webbed glass finally shattering, falling onto the seat.

Frost stuck the muzzle of the Metalifed High Power out the open window, over the jagged knife edges of glass, his left fist balled hard around the grips as he pumped the trigger toward the rifleman.

One shot, two, then two more and the slide locked open. The rifle discharged, the barrel swinging upward and a tongue of orange flame visible from the muzzle for an instant. Frost tossed his pistol onto the seat beside him, the subgunner opening up again. Frost wrenched the steering wheel hard left, then stomped the gas pedal, throwing himself across the seat as the Cadillac broadsided the Lincoln.

He could feel his body shake, his breath short, almost robbed from him as the impact came. There was a crunching of metal, a groaning, and Frost looked down—part of the firewall on the driver's side had buckled and had he stayed behind the wheel he would have lost his legs.

Frost pushed himself across the seat, wrenching open the front passenger door, half rolling, half sprawling out onto the grass, the locked-open slide High Power in his right fist as he stumbled away from the cars. He dumped the empty magazine, dropping to his knees in the grass as he rammed a fresh magazine in place.

His right thumb worked the slide release, the

slide running forward, stripping out the top round. Almost before the action was closed, Frost started to pump the trigger. The subgunner, bleeding, right arm stiff at his side, crawled from the back seat of the Lincoln—apparently where he'd been thrown—and with his weapon, an Uzi SMG, in his left hand, he started to fire. Frost fired, fired and fired again and again, the subgunner rocking with the hits, Frost's right fist knotted in a death grip on his pistol.

Frost's pistol stopped firing and the one-eyed man looked down at it—the slide was locked open, the front of the slide scorched dark brown and black.

The subgunner was sprawled, lifeless, across the accordioned hood of the Cadillac.

Frost got to his feet, finding his first empty magazine in the grass, pocketing it and starting to dump the empty magazine still in the Browning.

He sighed hard, turning around, seeing Oriana running up to him, red lines of blood splotched across her face and bare shoulders and the front of her dress.

"I'm sorry," Frost rasped. He rammed a fresh magazine into his pistol and let the slide close forward. He lowered the hammer on the Browning and reholstered it, starting around behind the Cadillac, toward the back seat of the Lincoln.

Frost stopped, looking inside. The face of the sniper was a bloody pulp. Frost wasn't certain if it was his gunfire or the crash. The rifle was there and Frost picked it up. The scope was twisted half off the mounts and the objective lens was shattered.

The gun was a .460 Weatherby Magnum.

Frost turned around to face Oriana, handing off the rifle to Alberto. He murmured to the man, "No wonder that thing did what it did—I'm surprised the glass held up at all."

Oriana was staring at him, and Frost repeated himself. "I'm sorry, Oriana—I liked your father."

She still only stared, then almost whispered, "Alberto—hit him!"

Frost started to turn, but only in time to see the upswinging butt of the bolt action rifle as it snaked toward his head.

Frost felt something, at once dull and sharp in the right side of his head, then there was only blackness . . .

Chapter Five

Frost felt something moving in his jacket pocket. He opened his eye. The face above him was gaunt, dirty, in need of a shave, the eyes wide, the pupils dilated.

It was like a face from a nightmare. Frost closed his eye, then felt hands on his chest.

Frost opened his eye again. A second face, almost a carbon copy of the first, this one above him, but upside-down seeming and then, suddenly, the face was gone—and replacing it against the blackish night sky was a white rock, held in a bony, dirt-stained hand.

Frost tried to roll away, but the hands on his chest held him down.

"Hurry it up—this sucker's big!"

Frost's left knee pulled up, finding the spot he wanted, then he let it down and snapped it up hard.

"Shit!"

Frost's hand went up, grabbing at the hand holding the rock above his head, the pressure from the hands on Frost's chest gone, but a body slumping across him now.

Frost tried to roll away again, but the hand with the rock was still pressing down above him, another hand starting to claw at his face. Frost released the grip with his left hand and snatched at the body across his chest, finding a handhold in a greasy-feeling head of hair, twisting the body away, then rolling as his hand gave way under the pressure of the hand from above him with the rock. The rock thudded down to the ground and Frost fell back on his knees, his right hand slapping under his coat for his pistol. It wasn't there. The man with the rock was coming at him now, the rock gone, but Frost's pistol in his left hand.

"I'm gonna kill you, mother—"

"Bite it, wimp," Frost snarled, pushing himself to his feet. His head ached and his vision blurred for an instant. But the man was still coming, the gun held low like an amateur would hold a knife.

"Knife," Frost rasped, finally forcing himself to think.

He reached under his coat, in the small of his back, the little Gerber still there.

The man was pulling the trigger of the High Power, but nothing was happening.

Frost pulled out his knife and took a quick half step forward, wheeling, knocking the gunhand aside with his left elbow and driving the little knife back and down, hard with his right fist.

"Aagh!"

The man behind him screamed and Frost saw the Browning fall to the ground.

Frost stepped away, turning, the one who'd been on his chest starting to get to his feet, holding his crotch with his right hand.

Frost took a half step and kicked with his right foot, the toe of his sixty-five dollar shoe catching the half-kneeling man at the base of the jaw, the head snapping back, the body sagging to the ground.

Frost stepped back, woozy, his head aching. He dropped his knife to the ground and felt with the fingers of his right hand along the right side of his head. Dried blood, and what felt like some sort of massive bump.

He shook his head, to clear it, but the pain almost made him pass out.

Frost dropped to his knees, picking up his knife. He crawled the few feet to the man he'd stabbed. He felt for a pulse, but there was none. Frost searched his own pockets, finding his Zippo, lighting it. He studied the man's face a moment, yellowish in the glare of the lighter's flame. The eyes, wide open in death, were dilated, discolored at the edges, as if bloodshot. Frost closed the lighter, to save the wick, then lifted the man's right arm, assuming him to have been left handed from the way he had held the gun. Frost lit the Zippo again, pushing up the dirty sleeve of the long-sleeved shirt the dead man wore.

"Tracks," the one-eyed man murmured in the darkness. "Damn junkie." Frost closed the dead man's eyes.

Frost found his gun in the dirt and dropped the magazine, checking the chamber, checking that the barrel wasn't fouled by blowing down it and listening for the hollow whistling noise, like the sound from blowing into an empty beer bottle. He reloaded his pistol, then checked the second man. The man's head was at an odd angle to the body. Frost felt near the neck—the neck was broken and there was no pulse. He closed the eyes of the second man, then inspected both arms. There were track marks everywhere.

Murmuring, "Yuch," he rolled back the eyelids of the second man—needle marks as well.

"Idiot," Frost whispered, shaking his head.

He searched his own pockets completely this time, finding his money clip and his wallet and cigarettes gone and all his spare magazines, except the one in the clip dump under his right arm.

He searched the pockets of the dead men, finding everything that was missing from his own pockets.

"Fine thing—can't even lie around unconscious without some damned junkie tryin' to roll ya," he complained to himself. "Talking to myself—head must be hurt more than I thought," he added. He lit a cigarette, his hands unsteady. He wiped the blade of his knife clean on the clothes of the man he'd stabbed, then resheathed it.

Frost pushed himself to his feet, putting the High Power back into the leather.

He looked down at his suit. Even in the semi-darkness, he could see it was stained.

He pulled out his wallet once more, lighting the Zippo again after he found the business card. "Lew Wilson, Florida Department of Law Enforcement." As soon as he figured out to which way lay civilization, he could find a phone booth and call Wilson—the home number was on the reverse side of the card.

Frost pocketed the card and the wallet, looked up at the stars and started walking in what he hoped was a northerly direction.

"Damn junkies," Frost murmured again.

Through the darkness, he could hear noises from what sounded like a road, maybe trucks speeding along it. After whoever it had been—Alberto? After

Alberto had slugged him with the rifle butt—"Ohh," Frost groaned, remembering suddenly all that had happened—the assassination of Moises Vasquez, the blood all over Oriana's face and shoulders and dress.

They had dumped him somewhere, Frost decided, or perhaps Oriana had ordered Alberto to kill him and Alberto had chosen otherwise.

Frost felt a smile crossing his lips, his head hurting with the muscle movement. There definitely was a road up ahead, past the palm trees. If Alberto had taken it on himself not to kill him—Frost—then Frost owed Alberto a favor. Otherwise, for the rifle butt across the side of his head, Frost owed the big Cuban a trip to the intensive care ward.

Chapter Six

"Hello, Lew?" Frost stared at the phone, still tired, slightly groggy and his head aching, as if waiting for the phone to nod back.

"God, man—Frost? It's two A.M.!"

"Congratulations—you tell time real good," Frost answered, glancing at his own left wrist and confirming Wilson's estimate of the hour.

"Second damn call in the last forty-five minutes—where the hell are you?"

"Second call—about me?"

"Yeah—nightwatchman on the door at our offices —somebody dumped a load of stuff out of a moving car in front of the place. Figured it was a bomb. Got Miami PD bomb squad over there—just a bunch of clothes, a box full of eyepatches and a KG-99—figured it was Oriana returning your things."

"Then you heard about this afternoon?" Frost asked.

"You look at a newspaper—damn right I heard about it. Eduardo Ruiz shot and killed, his bodyguards murdered, his car stolen, then used in the assassination of another Omega Seven leader— Vasquez. Where the hell you been?"

Frost looked around the hotel lobby. "Busy," he

finally said. "I'd tell you about it but you'd have to arrest me."

"What?"

"I'm at the hotel—whatever the hell name it is—the place I was staying when I first moved in—I mean before I moved in with the Vasquez's to guard Señor Vasquez—look, I dunno what the hell I mean," Frost finally said, lighting a cigarette. "Look—you wanna come over in about an hour?"

"No—but I will. You know, some people gotta work tomorrow."

"It's Saturday Lew—tomorrow—isn't it?"

"Oh—yeah—well, yeah; I'll be there. You all right?"

"No," and Frost hung up, figuring Wilson could get his room number from the desk.

Frost took the elevator to his floor, then let himself inside. He turned on the lights, stripping off his jacket and dropping it on the floor as he walked across the room. He stopped at the mirror over the low dresser and looked at himself.

He figured with luck he could salvage the tie, but not his head.

Frost stripped off the tie and set it on the dresser, then looked at the side of his head. He was black and blue, a heavy welt running up diagonally from his right cheekbone and disappearing into his hair line, the hair matted with blood. The trucker who had picked him up had told Frost that he'd thought the one-eyed man looked as though he'd been run over by a truck. Frost agreed, saying he felt that way.

Frost kicked off his sixty-five dollar shoes; these too he considered salvageable.

"Kiss off another suit," he murmured to himself, unzipping his pants and dropping them on the floor. He pulled off his shoulder rig, dropping it on the dresser. He ripped his shirt off—it was bloodstained, mudstained and grass stained—he thought he might send it to one of the detergent companies to see if it could make it in a TV commercial.

He decided the underpants could be saved. He dropped them. He started into the bathroom, turned on the light and leaned against the doorframe, pulling off his socks—they were okay, except for the hole near his right big toe, but that had been there before.

He sat down on the toilet, too tired to trust his aim, then urinated.

"Aww," he groaned, then stood up, walking to the telephone. He picked it up and dialed the operator.

"Operator."

"Gimme room service."

"You can dial room service directly, sir, but room service closed at one, sir."

"Gimme the bell captain, okay—or does he have his own number?"

"The bell captain does have his own number sir, but I can connect you—hold on please."

Frost waited, hearing a buzzing sound on the other end of the line—he thought the switchboard might have disconnected him. "Front."

"Rear," Frost smiled.

"What?"

Frost told the voice on the other end of the line, "Never mind—this is Mister Frost in," and he tried to remember his room number. "1407, I think—they got it at the desk. Look—room service is closed."

"Yes, sir," the voice agreed.

"Twenty bucks in it for you if you bring me up a bucket of ice, two glasses, a quart of Seagrams Seven and about four big cheeseburgers and some french fries — interested?"

"Yes, sir — that's Mr. Frost?"

"Yeah — only gimme a half hour — gonna take a shower."

"Yes, sir — twenty dollars, ice, glasses, Seagrams quart, four cheeseburgers and french fries. Yes, sir."

"In a half hour —"

"Right sir — twenty dollars —"

"Yeah," and Frost hung up. He walked back into the bathroom and stepped into the shower, surprised he made it when the water hit his head, but the pain was only, as he mumbled, ". . . mildly excruciating," and he closed his eye. It wasn't sleep that he wanted, it was something considerably more violent . . .

Chapter Seven

"Want some french fries, Lew? Little rubbery, but what the hell," Frost said, gesturing across the room as he stood in the open doorway, a hotel bathtowel around his waist. "Come on—I'll fix you a drink."

"At three A.M.?"

"Time is relative, Lew—on the West Coast, it's just midnight—and in Hawaii—"

"Aww, shut up Hank." And Wilson came inside and shucked off his coat, the Beretta 92SB stuffed in his trouser band.

Frost sat down on the edge of the bed, watching the television set. "I'd offer you a cheeseburger, but this is the last one and I already took a bite out of it."

"The bell captain's bringin' up your stuff—I stopped by the office first and—"

"He's gonna get rich off me tonight. You ever see this one?" and Frost gestured toward the television set.

"Yeah, I've seen it."

"Watch—now the President's gonna pull a rod on that guy and chase him—there—"

"Damnit, Hank!"

Frost looked up at his friend, saying, "Have a french fry, make yourself a drink and relax. In what other nation can you see the President at three in the

51

morning—I ask you that? What a glorious country we have."

"Are you drunk?"

"I never get drunk—not really. Used to a lot. But I told you about that once."

"What the hell happened to your face?"

"More the side of my head—but I'm okay," Frost nodded, watching the President.

"Hank?"

"Look—I learned a lot today. I learned a lot about people, about myself, about women even."

"What—when Moises Vasquez got killed?"

"Yeah—I learned a lot."

"You learn that Oriana Vasquez has assumed leadership of her father's branch of Omega Seven and declared open warfare on the pro-Castro people?"

"No—but I figured she would—he's a fine figure of a man, isn't he," Frost observed, gesturing toward the television set.

"Yeah—but did you realize that everything we tried setting up is all gone—And just when we had a line into the damn M-19—"

"Figured you'd get a line—best cop I know—I knew you would," Frost smiled, lighting a Camel.

"You're drunk."

"No," and Frost looked up at Wilson and stood up, walking over to the television set. "You watching this?"

"No—no," Wilson nodded.

"Good night, Sir," and Frost flicked off the tube. He looked at Wilson. "No—I just realized what I've gotta do."

"You're drunk," and Frost noticed Wilson eyeing the one-third empty bottle of Seagrams.

"No—really not much anyway—anyway, I'm tired, but that'll pass."

"Look, Hank—"

There was a knock at the door and Frost went to it, opening the door. It was the bellman with his things. "Leave 'em inside the door," and Frost reached beside the door and peeled off a five dollar bill from his money clip, giving it the bellman.

"Is there anything else, sir?"

"Yeah—send me a postcard when you take that vacation to the Bahamas," and Frost closed the door.

"What the—"

"My gun in there?"

"Yeah."

"Keep it for me and my stuff for a while—I'm goin' south, to Colombia."

"Colombia?"

"Yeah—if you can make me some connections, wonderful. If not, I'll go cold."

"Colombia—what for?"

"Gonna kill whoever it is in M-19 that helped knock off Moises Vasquez—was a good old guy," and Frost stubbed out his cigarette and returned to his cheeseburger.

"That's crazy."

"That's Hank Frost, Lew—you know that."

"Bullshit!"

"No—common sense. Old man Vasquez—he was right. There is a traitor in Omega Seven—and to find the traitor I've gotta nail the sucker that's the controller. Logic dictates that's in M-19. So, I go there."

"You're really bonkers, you know that?"

"Well, can't win 'em all—maybe it's the blow to the head, or the four cheeseburgers," and Frost downed the last bite, then leaned back, lighting another cigarette, his elbows resting on the bed. "But I'm not drunk, and I'm just ordinary tired, and my head hurts, but it's hurt worse and probably will again. No—nothin' wrong with me, Lew. I'm seeing this thing clearly for the first time since I got here."

"I'm gonna call your girlfriend Bess in London— maybe she can talk some sense into you—"

"You'd do it on my dime too—I know. But don't go callin' mommie just yet—hear me out. And anyway, I'm meetin' her stateside in two weeks. You can call her more reasonably then."

Wilson sat down, then stood up and poured himself a drink. "Goddamn three in the morning!"

"I'll drink to that," Frost smiled, taking a swallow of the whiskey. "No—see. See, Moises Vasquez had the right idea, but he didn't know how right he was. I'm surprised the traitor didn't kill me."

"Who?"

"Oriana," Frost murmured, lighting another cigarette.

"You're not drunk, you're not crazy—you're—"

"I know—words fail you," Frost smiled. "But it's Oriana. She was wearing this shawl—"

"Maybe she was cold."

"She dropped the shawl and bent to get it—just when her father was sniped."

"Aww, Hank—gee—that's dumb!"

"Lew—she's a Latin woman, brought up with some degree of wealth, a lady, gone to the best schools, the whole nine yards—"

54

"So?"

"You ever know a girl like that?"

"Yeah—a few times."

"Would she bend over to pick up her own shawl with her father a yard away from her, one of her father's bodyguards right beside him? Would she stoop over and pick it up—or would she wait for the man?"

"You know how far you'd get with that in court?"

"I don't need court—"

"What the hell are you sayin'?"

"I'm sayin' Oriana Vasquez nailed her father, set me up on it maybe—I don't know that yet. But she nailed him, probably nailed her stepmother. Under other circumstances, I'd put her away. But with you here, I can't do that—I don't want us on opposite sides. So I'm gonna find out. If I'm wrong, I'll go tell her I'm sorry—but if I'm right, you can arrest her."

"What if you're right but I can't arrest her?"

Frost inhaled hard on his cigarette, looking into his friend's face. "I don't know—Moises Vasquez—he was a good guy. Oriana—well, I think she's a double-crossing ice-cold bitch. I don't know."

"You sayin' she had the nerve to stand there while somebody splattered her father's brains all over her—God, man—"

"Would you suspect her, even if you had suspected her before?"

"No," Wilson murmured.

"That's why I do," Frost told his friend. "That's why I do."

The one-eyed man stubbed out the cigarette, then after a second, lit another one.

Chapter Eight

"Joe?"

"Joe," Wilson nodded, looking at Frost across the coffee cup.

"If there were another one, what would his name be?"

"Cut it out," Wilson laughed. "He just calls himself Joe—that's his business."

"Yeah," Frost nodded, drinking his coffee. "Guess it's better than Hank or Lew—crappy names like that, yeah—probably."

"Aww, Frost—"

Frost laughed, downing his coffee, catching the eye of the waitress and signalling for more. He looked at his eggs, then at his watch. It was noon. "Why not?" and he started to eat.

"I hadda pull a lot of strings to arrange this thing, Hank—even to get the okay to tell you the guy calls himself Joe."

"He's the top Federal drug cop?" Frost asked.

"Yes and no—he's the top man in their undercover operations—he's a sort of controller, more like you'd expect in an espionage set-up rather than law enforcement—but it's pretty much come to that in some ways. We spy on the crooks and sometimes they spy on us."

"So this Joe," Frost continued through a mouthful of fried eggs, "is the top spy, the spymaster?"

"In a manner of speaking," Wilson nodded, eating a piece of toast. "And he agreed to see you. You're gonna have to do the selling job if you want his help going against the M-19. I don't think he's gonna give it to you, myself. I don't think he'll trust a non-Fed with a lead this important."

"Yeah—but you think about it," Frost nodded, forking a piece of steak into his mouth, "a guy like me might be better than a cop for something like this. I'm more conditioned to shooting people rather than arresting people, I'm used to jungle fighting, things like that. Who knows, maybe he'll like the color of my eye, or maybe the color of my eyepatch," and Frost smiled, tugging at the black patch covering his face where his left eye would have been.

"You go down there Hank, after the M-19—with Joe's help or not, I don't think you're comin' back."

Frost put down his knife and fork for a moment, then looked across the table at Wilson. "Lew—when I went into Burma after those warlords in the opium trade,* that was one of the few times I really figured maybe I wasn't coming back. I told you about that. I could hardly walk, figured I was crippled for life—the whole shot. But I learned something. I guess I'd known it all along, and maybe that just made me become aware of it. You just never tell yourself to give up, and you don't. It makes the difference—really."

"Hank Frost the philosopher mercenary—neat,"

"I'm just a multi-faceted personality," the one-

---

*See, They Call Me The Mercenary #4, *The Opium Hunter*

eyed man smiled. He started working on the steak again . . .

A shoddily constructed fence—Frost couldn't guess at its purpose—ran like a falling-apart barricade along the hillocks of sand between the beach and the water, and standing there near the fence was a tall, thin-looking man. He wore a slouch hat, white, and dirt-stained white trousers with a light blue shirt. As Frost walked closer, he could see that the beard the man wore was more than half grey in the jowls."

"You Joe?"

"You Hank Frost?"

"Yeah."

"Then I'm Joe—come on—we'll walk a little."

Frost looked down at his sixty-five dollar shoes and shrugged—they were covered with sand anyway. "Okay—we'll walk—Joe."

"Good, Hank—this way."

Joe started to turn around, but Frost raised a hand, saying, "You mean—walk this way? Like the old vaudeville joke?" And Frost took two exaggerated pigeon-toed steps closer to Joe.

"You think you're funny, huh?"

Frost shrugged. "Better than takin' myself too seriously—you didn't like the joke, huh?"

"No."

"How about, why did two chickens cross the road?"

"That's old—why?"

"The chickens were star-crossed lovers who'd formed a suicide pact."

"You wanna talk or just make jokes?"

Frost smiled, starting to walk along the fence line, Joe falling in step with him. "I'll walk this way," the one-eyed man murmured.

58

"Shit—you come here with some cockamamie idea about knockin' off the head of M-19 and you go makin' with the jokes."

"When did you leave New York?"

"Ten years ago—it still shows that much?"

"I've got a good ear—for languages, accents, stuff like that."

"I was a narc up there, then came south."

"For your health?"

"Might say that—but it didn't turn out that way. Why should I trust you?"

"You got a lead as to where M-19 headquarters is—first lead you've ever had like that. But you can't have the Colombian army goin' in there and shootin' the place up, because likely they'll get a lot of the little bad guys and they won't get the top man, right?"

"You're the one doin' the talkin'—I'm listenin'."

"Terrific," and Frost lit a cigarette. "So—send me in. I'll get myself up there and find the right guy and put him away."

"You do—"

"Contract killing? Not on your life. This is for fun, not profit. See, I liked Moises Vasquez, and I figure the guy in M-19 is the guy who gave the order to kill Vasquez."

"Probably—so?"

"So, I'm just carrying out justice. He had Vasquez killed, well—now it's his turn. That's all."

"You figure," Joe asked, putting his hand in Frost's left arm, stopping him, looking at him, "that all you've gotta do is walk in there, introduce yourself, get pointed to the right guy and pull a trigger?"

"You check me out?"

"Yeah—I did."

"Then you know that's not the way I'll do it."

"Don't go guaranteeing results," Joe laughed. "Cause probably, all's gonna happen is you gettin' yourself knocked off."

"Look at it this way," Frost smiled, inhaling, then exhaling a cloud of grey smoke caught up in the mild breeze. "If you send a Fed to do this—and that's the only option you've got unless you wanna pass up the lead, throw it away. But if you send a Fed, and he gets caught, you've got a diplomatic incident on your hands, and a hell of a lot of flack from the people you work with in Colombia. But if you send me, and I get caught—hell—just some crazy one-eyed mercenary out on a vengeance trip. You can probably ruin my good name and turn it around to make it look like somebody in the drug business hired me to put the guy away. So you don't have anything to lose."

"You're crazy," Joe said with an air of finality. "And what, just hypothetically, do you want for doin' this? If you can do it?"

"Gimme a leather medal," Frost smiled.

"You got a deal—either way. We can always give ya a leather medal posthumously."

"I kill him, we stop the arms smuggling for a while, maybe for a long while and maybe even put a little crimp into the drug smuggling. Who knows?"

"I know," Joe smiled. "You're gonna get your ass in the wringer and I'm never gonna have to waste my time talkin' to ya again. You go ahead. I'll get you contacted—stay near your hotel phone. And don't tell Wilson or any of his friends in FDLE—this can be between us. Just tell 'em you're gonna go down there

60

and when they ask questions, give 'em the old line—"

"We're not allowed to say?"

"Yeah—and don't ever contact me again."

Joe turned around and walked away. Frost heeled out his cigarette in the sand and then did the same.

Chapter Nine

Frost studied what he saw through the taxi cab window as the vehicle crunched to an uneven stop. He had seen places like it in New York, and in Chicago. Los Angeles—all over the world. He wasn't quite certain what it was called, in Colombia. Perhaps a barrio—but in an English-speaking country, it would have been called a ghetto.

Frost paid the driver and got out, watching the faces there watching him. Behind him were narrow huts, with hungry looking children, half-naked and dirty, playing in the sewers in the potholed street. Before him was a vast open area, houses half-destroyed, old buildings partially torn down and here and there a piece of idle construction equipment.

Frost started toward the field of rubble, feeling the eyes of the children boring into his back, hearing the screech of wheels as the cab driver started away. It was infrequent that an American wanted to come here.

The meeting was with the person who was Joe's counterpart—the chief clandestine operative of the Colombian anti-drug/anti-terrorist force. Frost had thought it silly, when told by the Colombian authorities he'd been put in contact with: "You will know our agent by the pink rose—that is the way."

A pink rose? Frost wondered what sort of agent he was to meet. He picked his way across the piles of rubble and toward a falling-down board sign reading in part "Mercado." He froze, a tiny mechanical click behind him.

Slowly, he turned around, the little Gerber knife up his sleeve instead of in the small of his back where it was usually carried. As he moved his right arm, the knife slipped down into the cuff of his shirt and he had the butt of it in the palm of his hand. He absently thought he might have cut the inside of his forearm, just holding the knife there with a piece of twine, then flexing it free.

But the origin of the little mechanical clicking sound, despite the fact that it was a gun, didn't cause him to bring the knife out into play. There was a woman, a beautiful one. And in her almost black hair was a flower—a pink rose.

"You are Capitan Frost?" she asked, the muzzle of the Heckler & Koch P-7 never moving.

"Yes."

"I am Miranda Ceballos."

"A lady drug cop—or is that just a clever disguise?"

"You will never find out," she said flatly, hitching up the midcalf-length print skirt she wore and placing the H-K 9mm into a leg holster high on her left calf.

"I already decided—it's not a clever disguise."

"And you—the eyepatch is, how do you say it—for real?"

"Unfortunately," Frost nodded.

"I am to lead a one-eyed man into the jungle to find M-19 headquarters. The thought does not thrill me."

"You'll learn to like me," Frost smiled. "I'm that

kind of a guy—honest," and he winked at her.

She started walking, or better, perhaps, picking her way across the rubble, Frost thought, as he had done a moment earlier. He followed along beside her. "I will provide you with all the equipment you will need—do you prefer a submachinegun or an assault rifle?"

"Assault rifle—M-16 preferably, or any of the H-K guns."

"We will travel by four wheel drive Jeep for part of the way—then we will walk. I might warn you," and she stopped walking, turned and faced him. "It is not only the M-19 that is dangerous where we go. It is the jungle, the mountains, the people who live there—all this can kill someone who doesn't know how to survive out there."

"Gee—I wish you hadn't told me that," Frost smiled. "Now I'll be too scared to go to sleep tonight."

"You had better fear, Capitan—for otherwise, you will die even sooner."

"You always this encouraging?"

"I have not been told why you are here, what you hope to gain by finding the M-19. I work hard at what I do and some damned American comes here and wants me to be his tour guide. I do not like it."

"That pink rose is very becoming," Frost smiled.

She pulled it from her hair and slapped him in the face with it, then started walking away. "I will be at your hotel with a plain car tomorrow morning at six—be ready and try not to look conspicuous," she shouted, walking away.

"Hey—you got a car?" Frost shouted. "I got rid of my taxi-cab."

"That is your misfortune."

Under his breath, the one-eyed man muttered, "Bite it, lady!"

Chapter Ten

"No—close your eyes now," Frost smiled as he began stripping away his white shirt.

"Idiot," Miranda Ceballos snapped, climbing from the driver's seat and standing along the roadside. Frost stuffed the shirt into the top of his pack and found a camouflage fatigue blouse and pulled it on. He did the same with the summerweight slacks he'd worn from the hotel, and with his sixty-five dollar shoes, skinning into jungle-pattern fatigue pants and a pair of black, GI combat boots.

Frost stepped out of the car. "Now where?" he called out, slipping into the Cobra Comvest shoulder rig, then going around to the already open trunk for his rifle.

"Now, a little walk—and then the Jeep and we are moving."

"Super," Frost smiled. He checked the M-16, working the action several times, then broke it open on the pivot pin, withdrawing the bolt. He inspected it minutely—he disliked taking a gun which he had never fired before into a possible combat situation. But the assault rifle appeared normal. He replaced the bolt, then closed the weapon, checking the action again several times, then snapping off the trigger, closing the dust cover and inserting a thirty-round magazine up the well.

He buckled on the web belt with his canteen and other gear, then took the small musette bag with the spare magazines for the M-16 and slung it from right shoulder to left hip, cross body. He did the same with the Bushnell 8x30 armoured binoculars, slinging them left to right, then went back to the front passenger seat for his pack and his cammie pattern slouch hat.

"Ready when you are, Miranda," Frost shouted. "What about the keys to the car?"

"It will be picked up," she said with an air of impatience, then started off into the brush, an M-16 slung across her back beside her pack. A short-sleeved cammie pattern T-shirt and bush shorts with high stockings and combat boots was all she wore.

"It will be picked up," Frost repeated mockingly. Somehow, Miranda Ceballos reminded him of Oriana Vasquez—and that Frost didn't like . . .

The walk to the Jeep had been a mile, as best Frost could judge it, the terrain rough walking but nothing, he realized, compared to the jungle ahead. For the most part, there would be roads to follow toward the mountains, then the walking would begin, but by then the jungle would be mostly behind them. In all, the journey itself, at least as far as the terrain was concerned, didn't worry him. The uncommunicative Miranda Ceballos, the M-19 terrorists between where they had boarded the Jeep and the mountain stronghold—these bothered him, as did what he would do when he got there.

The one-eyed man smiled, leaning back in the passenger seat of the Jeep, watching the scrub brush race past the vehicle on both sides. Maybe "Joe" had been right—it was a fool's errand . . .

"I must urinate—wait for me," Miranda Ceballos snapped, wrenching the stick into neutral and then applying the emergency brake. She climbed down from the open Jeep without another word, then started into the bush.

Frost shrugged, lighting a cigarette in the blue-yellow flame of his battered Zippo. He started to reach over to shut off the key, but didn't, wondering if perhaps there were some reason she had left the motor running. On impulse more than anything else, Frost worked the rabbit-eared bolt handle of the M-16, chambering the top round out of the magazine, then setting the selector to safe. He kept the rifle, muzzle up, between his knees, listening to the jungle sounds around him.

Frost glanced at the black faced Rolex, noting the time. It seemed as though she'd been gone too long. He smiled, saying half aloud, "Women take a long time, but . . ." He climbed down from the Jeep. He looked into the back of the Jeep. She had left her M-16. "Hmm," the one-eyed man murmured.

Then he wheeled 180 degrees, thrusting the muzzle of the M-16 ahead of him, flicking the selector to full auto. There was someone running through the brush, toward him. "Capitan Frost—Capitan!"

The runner broke through the foliage and Frost could see—it was Miranda Ceballos, still zipping the front of her bush shorts, running, mouth wide open gulping air, her eyes wide—but with fear.

There was more noise from the jungle behind her and Frost shouted, "What the—"

"M-19—terrorists," and she was onto the road now, still running.

Frost jumped aboard the Jeep, throwing it into reverse as he released the emergency brake, then zig-zagging the Jeep back toward her. He screeched to a halt, the transmission sticking as he tried for first. She was jumping aboard—he could see her out of the corner of his eye. He wrenched the stick into second and rode the clutch as he fed the gas, the Jeep jerking forward. Frost glanced behind him now. Breaking from the jungle foliage he could see men, two, two more, then three more, faces cammie-makeup-patterned, clothes cammie patterned and Soviet type AKM assault rifles in their hands. "Holy—" Frost tried downshifting into first, and finally he got the trans-mission into the fork, the Jeep stuttering, then shoot-ing ahead. Frost hauled up the assault rifle, holding it in his left hand, awkwardly moving the selector back onto full auto—he had moved it when boarding the Jeep.

"What are you—"

"Shut up," Frost snarled, balancing the wheel of the Jeep with his left knee, his right heel punching the clutch as he shifted back into second, the toes of his right foot working the gas as well now.

He levelled the M-16 behind the Jeep, toward the M-19 terrs, pumping the trigger.

"No—they'll—"

"Shut up, damnit!" Frost shouted, firing the M-16 in short bursts. "Start shooting!"

His first burst cut down the lead man, but the others were still coming, running down the road after the Jeep, firing. The windshield shattered, and bullets whined as they ricocheted off the body work. Frost kept firing. "Start shooting Miranda!"

The woman beside him reached into the back of the Jeep, grabbing up her M-16, working the bolt, then shouldering the rifle as she twisted in the seat into a better position.

Frost glanced away then, firing the M-16 empty in his left fist, missing the running terrorists by yards because of the awkward way in which he held the rifle.

"Hell!" the one-eyed man rasped, dropping the empty rifle beside him. Awkwardly, left handed, Frost wrenched the Metalifed High Power from the leather, jerking back the hammer and firing the pistol. He hit the nearest of the terrorists with the first two-round semi-auto burst, the man's body plopping into the road, lost then in the dust the Jeep was making in its backwash.

Frost upped the safety and set the pistol across his lap, taking hold of the wheel again with his left hand, working the transmission with his right, both feet on the pedals now. He had the slow-moving vehicle into third, and it was groaning ahead.

"Look out!" he shouted, seeing movement in the foliage to their left , ahead of the Jeep along the roadside.

Frost snatched up the High Power again, pointing it forward along the frame edge of the shattered windshield, firing. A man was coming from the brush, an assault rifle in his hands. At least one of Frost's shots impacted—the one-eyed man could see the result—the terrorist's head snapping back, a bright flower of blood where the nose should have been.

More men were coming, and Frost shouted to the

girl, "Ahead of us—get them!"

Frost cut the wheel hard right, away from the blazing assault rifles of the M-19 terrs, across the narrow rutted road, the Jeep bouncing high and crashing down over a ridge of dirt bordering the road, the impact bone-shattering. Frost leaned out of the Jeep, the High Power in his left fist, firing. The slide locked back empty then, the M-19s still pursuing on foot, still shooting. "Shoot, damn you!" Frost yelled to the girl.

She opened fire, the angle of the muzzle high as Frost looked toward her.

"Lady!" Frost glared at her, wrenching the wheel into a hard left across the scrub brush as the first group of M-19s were catching up, firing, trying to cut him off. Frost reached across the woman and grabbed at the pistol belt at her waist, wrenching it around so he could grab at the tiny flap holster there. He ripped the holster open, snatching the H-K P-7 from the leather, the woman trying to grab his wrist.

Frost loosed the gun for an instant and backhanded her across the face, snapping her head back. He grabbed the pistol again, his right fist squeezing around it. Pointing the gun across the front seat as the terrs closed, his fingers depressed the safety/cocking mechanism and he fired, the P-7 rocking in his hand. The nearest of the terrorists—twenty yards away and running hard a split second earlier—hit the dirt, his legs knocked from under him as Frost's round impacted, the man's hands going to his crotch. Frost turned the pistol to his left. The terrs who had tried cutting him off along the roadside were coming, the lead man less than a dozen yards from the Jeep. Frost fired, a bright splotch of blood appearing in the center of the man's forehead. Frost rasped to himself, "Lucky shot."

The one-eyed man stuffed the pistol into his trouser belt, wrenching the gear shift, downshifting into first, cutting the wheel into a tight left arc, aiming the Jeep at the nearest of his pursuers. He upshifted into second, taking the P-7 again, firing once, then once again. Another of the terrs went down. The ridge of dirt was ahead, and then the road. Frost dropped the pistol on the seat beside him, downshifted and gave the Jeep all the gas he could, the Jeep rocking up over the ridge. The one-eyed man cut the wheel hard right, upshifting, the terrs all behind him now. He hauled into third, then glanced to his right.

Miranda Ceballos had the P-7 in her right fist, aimed at his head.

Chapter Eleven

"Feelings hurt—what? Tell me," Frost asked, his voice low, his fists locked onto the steering wheel. "And while you're at it, tell me why you didn't try killing any of those bastards—they were sure as hell trying to kill us."

"You don't understand things here," she snapped, almost spitting out the words.

"Bullshit—people shoot at you, you shoot back."

"I—you are a fool. You could have gotten us killed back there, and you may still."

"Why are you pointing that gun at me—you gonna use it?"

"I don't know," she answered evenly.

"Just keep in mind that a high speed collision with a tree in an open vehicle isn't too much fun, and if you pull that trigger, that's just what you're gonna have," Frost rasped, glancing at her, then looking back up the road. "Now put the gun away, or I'll pick a nice, unfriendly looking tree."

"You are crazy."

"Put it away," Frost snarled, cutting the wheel hard left for an instant, just missing a towering tree that stood by the side of the road.

"No!"

"Put the gun away! Now!"

"You wouldn't!"

"Angry men do a lot of things most people think they wouldn't—now! Or the next tree we pass won't be a miss!"

Their eyes met, the girl's eyes tight, angry, and, he noticed for the first time, almost coal black.

"Well?"

The girl lowered the pistol, then slid it into the holster. "All right—but you're insane."

"Don't forget it," Frost almost whispered, slowing down, the terrorists long since vanished from the rear view mirror.

"What do you plan to do?"

"Find the M-19 camp—in one piece when I do. But before that," and Frost stomped the pedal and threw the transmission down, wrenching the wheel hard right, the Jeep fishtailing, skidding. Frost reached for the girl with his right hand, grabbing her hair at the nape of the neck, pulling her head back. As the Jeep lurched to a halt, his left hand snatched back the pistol.

He let go of her hair, his voice low as he said, "Now get out of the Jeep—move!"

The girl's cheeks were red, with rage, Frost guessed, but she obeyed him, climbing down from the vehicle. Frost shoved the P-7 into his belt, found his own High Power and changed magazines, then let the slide go forward, chambering the first round. He lowered the hammer, then holstered the pistol.

He climbed down from the Jeep and started walking toward her, saying, "I'm sure there's a perfectly logical reason why you ran like hell from those guys, but didn't want to shoot at them. Did you get to urinate?"

"Yes," she answered, her tone one of disgust.

"I'm glad for you. Now—tell me what's going on. And quick, or I'll leave you here."

"You wouldn't leave me," and she gestured to the jungle on both sides of the road, "here. I know you wouldn't."

"Try me," Frost told her. "You play straight with me, and I'll go to bat for you any time, any place. You cross me, and you've got trouble. What'll it be?"

"All right—but give me back my gun."

"Why—all you do is point it at me."

"Give me back my gun!" she screamed.

"When you tell me what's going on—just why the hell you didn't shoot at those guys. Now!"

"All right—it's a, a long story. And you might not believe it," she began.

"Try me," and Frost leaned back against the right front fender of the Jeep, waiting.

"They trust me—most of them—the M-19."

"Well, it's always good to trust a cop."

"Shut up, will you—you asked me to—"

"Go ahead," and Frost pushed himself away from the Jeep and walked around behind it, fishing into his pack. He found what he wanted, the box of 115-grain JHPs he'd packed along there. Then he opened the box. As Miranda began to talk, he began reloading the empty magazine for his Browning, listening.

"The reason I've been so effective working against M-19 is because they think I work with them—some of them do, at least. I was afraid that if I shot at any of those men, they might pass the word back to M-19 headquarters and my effectiveness would be destroyed."

"Not to be vulgar," Frost smiled, "but baloney."

"It is not sausage!"

Frost just looked at her, saying nothing.

"It is true. I learn the movements of the M-19 and the drug smugglers because they think I am a drug smuggler. How do you think I planned to get us through this country and into their camp? My background as a drug smuggler—a small-time one—is known, and I quickly built a background for you. You will appear to be a smuggler as well now—I can give them the background on you, to make it sound believable. That is your only chance for getting in there alive—let alone getting out again. And God help me when you try to get your man arrested or whatever it is that you plan, because I'll still have to help you and still make it appear as though I am one of them. And that is why I did not wish to shoot."

Frost lit a cigarette, putting away the box of ammo, securing the now reloaded magazine back into the offside pouch of the Cobra Comvest, the spine of the magazine facing forward. "You expect me to believe that?"

"I don't know really whether you will believe this or not," and she turned away and Frost thought that the little sniffing sound he heard might have been tears starting . . .

Chapter Twelve

There was someone playing a flute, a high-pitched rhythm that sounded to Frost unalterably primitive, yet strangely beautiful. Faces turned, staring, women grinding grain, others making tortilla-like pancake-shaped pieces of dough, half-naked children playing around them and dogs yelping at the heels of the children. The children were now running behind the Jeep as Frost turned down from the trail and into the single open area between the huts—the "main street" of the village.

"We can trust these people," Miranda Ceballos murmured. It was the first thing she had said other than to give navigational directions since their argument.

"Why—have you dealt with them before?" Frost asked her, still listening to the sound of the flute, still unable to detect its point of origin.

"I haven't—but I know others who have. They live off the smuggling trade too—they provide a halfway house for a lot of the smugglers working their way up into the mountains. Not just drugs, but raw uncut emeralds. They're illegal to export."

"So of course some people find ways of exporting them," Frost nodded. "Make something illegal and someone's certain to find a need to have it, do it or use it."

"I guess that's why there are people such as ourselves, isn't it," she asked, apparently not expecting an answer, turning away from him and looking into the village street. The one-eyed man downshifted into first gear, mentally debating whether or not to tell Miranda Ceballos that he wasn't like her—a cop. He decided against it. He had no idea how strong her alleged ties with the M-19 might be, nor how she might feel about his desire to murder its head. He let it go.

Frost slowed the Jeep, coming to a stop in the approximate center of the widest portion of the street—what was likely the village square.

At the same instant, the children who had been running behind the Jeep began swarming over it. Frost stopped a light-fingered boy who looked about five or six—the boy was snatching the bayonet for Frost's M-16. "Easy, chief," the one-eyed man murmured. "Salte, amigo," and Frost held the little boy over the side of the Jeep and let the boy jump to the ground.

A little girl was reaching for Frost's backpack—the pack seemed bigger than she was. Frost, good-naturedly, smiled, "Deme eso, ninnia," then gently pushed her away.

"You speak Spanish," Miranda remarked.

"A little—enough to get by, usually. Who's the head honcho around here? You know?"

"No," she murmured, shaking her head, peering across the sea of children's faces.

Frost stood up, seeing a man's face in the crowd. Gesturing toward him, Frost began, "Ayudeme, por favor. Quien es—"

"I am in charge here, señor—and I speak well English."

Frost nodded, saying, "Hell of a lot better than my Spanish. We're looking for a place to put up for the night—understand you people do that sort of—"

"Si—you are a—well, you are?"

The man's eyes lit up. Frost nodded, "Yes—we're traders, so to speak."

"Si, traders. Esta bien!" Then he clapped his hands and spoke in Spanish so rapidly Frost had no chance of following. The one-eyed man turned to Miranda, asking, "What's he saying—I lost him after the first word."

"He's ordering some of the women to prepare food, and some of the other men to guard our Jeep from the children. But take anything valuable with you just in case."

Frost nodded, grabbing up his pack, his rifle and his bayonet. He shoved the bayonet in the pack and slung the rifle across his right shoulder as he stepped down from the Jeep. He reached back inside, snatching the keys. "Should I get the battery?"

Miranda Ceballos merely looked at him, then climbed down herself from the Jeep, on the opposite side. Around him were small children, shouting, "Cigarettes!"

Frost looked at a four-year-old girl, clinging to his right leg. She was shouting for cigarettes louder than any of the others. The one-eyed man just shook his head. He had met children like that before, and asking for cigarettes was relatively innocent compared to what some of them wanted or offered . . .

"Chicha—real good," the village chieftain, Frankie," offered, extending a metal cup to Frost. Frost took the cup and looked at it. The smell was definitely alcohol, so he figured it would sterilize the cup if he drank from it.

"Thank you," Frost nodded, taking a sip of the drink. The inside of his throat felt scorched as it went down.

Miranda Ceballos smiled, saying, "A poor people's drink—it is strong."

"Strong," Frost nodded.

"Si—fuerte," "Frankie" agreed.

There were bowls in front of them, and Frost took one and reached toward one of the common pots in the center of the mat on the dirt floor of the hut. "Peppercorns—beware," Miranda advised.

Frost glanced at her, then at the mixture inside the bowl.

"That is Ajiaco—better for you," she told him. "Boiled meat, carrots, potatoes and cream. You might not like the taste of the cream."

"Better than the peppercorns," Frost smiled, ladling some of the Ajiaco into his bowl, then picking up a wooden spoon and starting to eat. She was right—he didn't like the cream taste, but he ate anyway, hungry.

Frankie said little throughout the meal. And Frost watched him—not really trusting the man. There was such a thing as being too accommodating, too pleasant, Frost thought. His distrust went far enough that he had intentionally not drunk any of the Chicha until Frankie had drunk from the same bottle. The one-eyed man had no desire to awaken groggily in the

"Si—he was killed. By smugglers. That was not a lie."

"I'm sorry—lo sciento," Frost murmured.

"We must sleep," she said pulling away from him.

Frost looked over his shoulder toward the door of the hut, then at the watch on his left wrist. "You notice Frankie's watch?"

"No—should I have?"

"Yeah," Frost smiled. "This watch I wear—Rolex Oyster Perpetual Sea-Dweller. Costs about a grand, more or less."

"What does that have to do with Frankie?"

"He was wearing pretty much the same watch—but every other link in the band was gold. Shoots the price a lot higher."

"I don't—" Miranda began.

"Where the hell does a guy living here get a watch like that?"

"Could have been a gift, I suppose—from one of the smugglers."

"Yeah—could have been. Could have been something else though," and Frost reached beside him on the ground and pulled the Metalifed High Power from his shoulder rig, then began to check its condition of readiness. "Could have been almost anything, maybe. But could have been that he killed whoever wore it here and kept it for himself. He was wearing a gun—you see it?"

"Many people wear guns."

"You ever see a guy like him with a Gold Cup—Colt Gold Cup? With Tiffany style grips?"

"You mean he robs—"

"Yeah. I betchya he's got a terrific collection of old

Jeeps stored out there in the jungle, probably got an arms cabinet that looks like the gun department at the biggest shop in Miami. I think I figured out how he makes a living. Kills some of his guests. Not all of them, or else no one'd ever come. Just enough to keep himself well off."

"But why would he kill us?"

"See, when I was looking at his stuff, I started doing it because he was looking at mine. And we're small time, independents, right? Not with a big organization that can put the arm on him for killing us. Who's gonna complain if a couple of independent drug dealers get zapped."

"If you are right—but I do not think so. But—if you are right? What shall we do?"

"Wait a minute," and Frost stood up, slipping the shoulder rig on, then holstering his gun as he went to the doorway, parting the blanket from its edge and looking into the village square. Six men guarded the Jeep, all of them armed with rifles and machetes. He could see no one outside their hut, but automatically assumed it was being watched.

He walked back to the girl. "What do we do? We have a sleepless night—at least I do. Half-dozen guys surrounding the Jeep out there. If we make a break for it, we'll never reach the Jeep and we'll have God knows how many armed men on us. They'll come to us. A man and a woman alone, in the jungle, a little liquored up," Frost lifted the fresh bottle of Chicha and pulled the cork. He sniffed it. "Smells different. Could be poison, more likely some kind of native equivalent of a Mickey Finn. And—"

"A Mickey Fine?"

"Finn—Mickey Finn—you know, knock-out drops. Probably figure we made love, got drunk and went to sleep—or will have by the time they arrive."

"I would not—"

"I wasn't askin' you to," Frost told her dispassionately. "So—they probably plan on hitting us just before dawn—best time. Whatever we did, we should be out by then. Come in and kill us."

"Kill—"

"Probably the machetes—or maybe strangle us or smother us."

"But—"

"They won't be expecting us to be awake, and to be expecting them. Go to sleep." And Frost crouched down beside the woman, taking the M-16 and placing it across his lap. "Go to sleep—and grab some Z's for me while you—"

"Z's?"

"Never mind," and the one-eyed man lit a Camel in the blue-yellow flame of his battered Zippo windlighter. He was tired, wanted sleep badly, but wanted life even more . . .

He couldn't tell if he had been asleep, or his eye had merely closed for an instant, but the noise he heard was definite, distinct. A voice, outside the hut. Frost glanced at his watch—it would be sunrise soon.

He leaned across to the girl, saw her eyelids fluttering. "Dreaming," he murmured, then shook her, rousing her, his left hand clamping tight over her mouth as her eyes opened. He nodded toward the door, then with his right hand pointed to his mouth, then to his right ear, nodding back toward the doorway. She closed her eyes tight for a moment, then nodded, and Frost let go of her mouth.

He handed her the M-16 she had carried into the hut, pointing to the chamber, then to the selector. It was on safe. He had loaded the chamber earlier in the evening. She looked at the weapon and nodded, already on her feet, her boot laces untied. She cinched the belt around her waist, the belt that held up her bush shorts, then picked up her pistol belt. The buckle started to rattle and Frost put a finger to his lips, signalling silence.

He affixed his own web belt and shrugged into his packstraps and his slouch hat. The M-16 was in his hands, the bayonet in place, the selector set on safe.

The girl pulled on her pack and Frost pointed toward the opposite side of the doorway. Slowly, quietly, she moved toward it, dropping down into a crouch then and tying her boot laces.

Frost could hear the voice again, louder this time because he was closer to the doorway. He waited. Immediately after the girl had gone to sleep he had checked the hut. There was no other door, and the only window was shuttered closed and there was no crack large enough to see through, to tell they were up and awake when they should have been in a stuporous sleep.

He heard a second voice, then the rattle of steel against steel—someone unsheathing a knife.

They were coming, Frost realized. He felt it—in the pit of his stomach where his guts churned, in the palms of his hands where they sweated, in the first finger of his right hand where it twitched outside the trigger guard of the Colt-made assault rifle. With his right thumb, as quietly as he could, he moved the selector to full auto, and pointed to it for the girl to do the same. She nodded and he watched as she did, the clicking sound almost imperceptible—he hoped.

He saw the blanket stir in the doorway. A wind?

It stirred again. It wasn't the wind.

Frost took a half step back, closer to the wall. He realized that if the villagers and Frankie, their leader, were planning to use guns, it could have been suicide to stand where he stood—gunfire would penetrate the wall of the hut easily. But Frost gambled that there was no desire to repair the hut after each set of hapless visitors was murdered in their sleep. There would be an easier way. He glanced across to the dirt floor where they should have been sleeping and wondered how many times the dirt had been tilled to cover blood. Perhaps the victims were even buried under it. That would have been the most economical way.

The thought gave him shivers. He had been sitting on dead men.

Frost glanced at his watch, not worrying about the time, but thinking about the woman who had insisted that he buy it—Bess. A smile crossed his lips. He'd get back to her this time too, he promised himself—and Frankie wasn't going to have a second Rolex—ever again.

The blanket moved once more, and a face peered inside, ahead of it and below it the tip of a machete.

There was a scream. "Francisco!"

Frost stepped into the doorway and fired through the blanket, all that he could see of the face, and the tip of the machete. The eyes widened in terror and the man who'd shouted for Frankie fell away.

Frost took a half step back as two men came

through the blanket-covered doorway, two of the men from the Jeep outside—either the men or the guns were in short supply, Frost thought. He recognized the guns more than the men. Frost fired his M-16, the first man, an AK-47 in his hands, spinning out and falling to the ground, the second man starting to fire but a burst of gunfire from Miranda's M-16 almost cutting his head from his neck, the man going down.

"Hit the dirt," Frost shouted, reaching out and grabbing the woman and instead of hitting the floor of the hut, pulling her toward the wall nearest him, shielding her body with his arms as gunfire poured through the doorway and the walls of the hut. He'd miscalculated, but only a little, he told himself.

"Salga, Frost—con sus manos arriba!"

Frost recognized the voice—Frankie.

"Tire al suelo su arma, Frost!"

"He wants you to throw down your weapon," the girl in Frost's arms whispered.

The one-eyed man only nodded.

He smelled something—and it momentarily terrified him. The hut was made of something like straw, held together with mud. What he smelled was burning gasoline.

For some reason, in the next instant, he found his mind preoccupied with trying to remember the right word in Spanish. "Incendio," he murmured.

The girl looked up at him, her black eyes wide, rimmed with white, the pupils tight black dots. "When I say so, fire into that wall opposite the doorway—keep firing until your stick runs out."

"What?"

"The magazine—do as I say," Frost ordered.

88

The smell of burning gasoline was stronger now, and Frost could hear a crackling sound—he looked above him. The roof was aflame. "Bastards," Frost rasped.

He turned and fired a burst through the doorway, then aimed his weapon at the far wall of the hut, smoke already starting to make his eye tear, to make him cough.

"Now—Miranda! Now!"

The one-eyed man opened fire, and the girl standing beside him opened fire as well, hot brass shell casings from their rifles filling the air like hail, but burning hail, pelting at Frost's hands and face, some of the casings dropping down inside the open front of his shirt, the noise of the gunfire in the small space of the hut deafening.

But the wall was sheering away, disintegrating under the impact of the automatic weapons fire.

Frost's gun was empty and he loaded a fresh magazine. As Miranda's gun emptied, Frost ran the few paces to the wall and kicked at it with his left foot, then his right. Chunks started to give way. Frost looked above him—the ceiling of the hut was a raging inferno now, flames licking downward, chunks of the roof itself falling, burning on the floor. Frost snatched up the bottle of Chicha from the floor. He'd planned ahead and he smiled as he thought of it. Not bothering with his cigarette lighter, he held the crude wick of cloth he'd made for the Chicha bottle to a piece of flaming roof debris, the wick lighting.

"Look out," Frost rasped, hurling the improvised Molotov cocktail through the opening in the wall, then grabbing the girl by the hand, hugging her against him near the wall while he waited for the explosion.

There was a low roar, and several screams from outside the hut. "Come on," he shouted over the crackling of the fire and the roar of gunfire from all sides of the hut. The girl beside him, he stormed through the opening in the wall, into the grey dawn outside.

The entire village was up, guns, machetes, weapons of every description in their hands, ringed around the hut. Except for the one spot where Frost had thrown the Chicha Molotov cocktail. Frost shouted to the girl—"Follow me—hurry," and started to run.

He heard the scream from behind him. "The Jeep! What about the Jeep?"

"Forget it," Frost shouted back, firing a burst from the M-16 at a small row of men armed with shotguns and machetes. There was gunfire everywhere around him as he reached the jungle at the edge of the village, the broad green leaves shredding under it, hammering sounds as slugs tore into tree trunks. He glanced once behind him—the girl was coming, running hard, and firing at their pursuers.

Frost slowed, letting the girl get ahead of him, shouting to her, "Hurry up—I'll hold 'em off a little," and as Frost wheeled around a man was running toward him, a machete high in the air over his head, a wild-eyed look on his face, and his mouth open in a scream.

There was no time to elevate the muzzle of the M-16 to shoot. Frost rammed the gun up in a broad arc, the bayonet catching the man in the abdomen and ripping up into the chest until Frost pulled it out.

Another man, this one with a shotgun in his hands,

was coming. The man stopped, raised the shotgun to fire. Frost fired his M-16, spraying it into the man's chest and midsection, bringing him down.

Two more men were coming and Frost fired into them, bringing one man down, screaming and holding his crotch, the second man dodging into the jungle.

The one-eyed man pulled back behind a tree trunk, waiting. He felt something, wheeled and raised the M-16, blocking a chop from a machete with the front handguard, falling back against the tree trunk, the man with the machete coming at him again.

The fighting space was too tight for Frost to bring the muzzle of the M-16 around. He blocked the machete again, but this time with the edge of his bayonet, twisting the blade away from the machete and slicing downward with it, across the carotid artery of his attacker's neck. The man fell back, blood spraying to Frost's face.

Frost wheeled, the man who'd hidden in the jungle coming at him now, a shotgun in his hands. Frost dove to the ground as the shotgun discharged, the leaves above him and around him shredding. Frost fired his M-16, catching the man in the chest.

Frost pushed himself up to his knees, making to fire the M-16. It was empty, and three more men were coming, two with machetes and one with a rifle.

The one-eyed man snatched the Metalifed High Power from the Cobra Rig under his left armpit, jacking back the hammer, firing before he could get the sights up to eye level. The man with the rifle spun on his heels and fell flat, the body lost in the jungle foliage.

One of the men with the machetes was nearly on him and Frost fired again, this time the pistol up to eye level, the shot going clean into his attacker's neck, the man still coming, the feet moving but the eyes dead, the body crumpling to the ground less than a yard from where Frost crouched.

The second man with a machete stopped, the machete going down to his side, a curious look on his face as he raised his left hand, palm outward.

Frost shot him in the face, then started to run.

It was easy following Miranda through the jungle in the grey light, easy because of the speed with which she was moving, just as easy as it would be for the men following Frost to keep to his trail.

But there was another fear in Frost now—what if Miranda were not to be trusted, and were waiting for him? Or what if she mistook him—for only a second—for one of the villagers? He pushed the thought out of his mind, the Browning shoved in the waistband of his fatigue pants, his hands working as he ran to change sticks in the M-16.

He stopped running for an instant, looking behind him. Three men, and more behind them. Frost fired a short burst, cutting down one of them, the others returning fire, more of the leaves and branches around him withered under it. He started to run again.

They would pursue until he killed them all, the one-eyed man realized—they had no choice. If Frost or the girl lived and made it out of the jungle, the village would be targeted, by the drug smugglers, perhaps by the police. Frost kept running, his lungs aching with it. "Pick 'em up, lay 'em down," he ordered himself aloud, gasping for breath. "One more step—one more step—one more step—pick 'em up," and he kept running.

He dodged a half-rotted tree fallen across his path, jumped a deadfall tree trunk beyond it and fell, wheeling, the Browning in his fist, the safety down. There was someone behind the tree trunk—Miranda, her pistol in her right hand, her face ashen colored.

"They are still—"

"They—they are—aww hell—yeah," and Frost wriggled up beside her, behind the termite infested tree trunk.

"I—can't," she gasped.

Frost nodded, not wanting to speak, not knowing if he could.

He reholstered the High Power and raised the muzzle of the M-16. They would be coming. He knew that.

"One chance," he gasped. "One—gimme your rifle. Take your pistol. Run that way. I'll wait here—when they come—I'll backshoot 'em."

"No—what if—"

"Do it—now," he snarled, snatching her M-16 from her. She looked at him, her eyes wide with fear, wary. "It's trust time, kid—you trust me that I don't leave you here and split. Now move it."

Roughly—too roughly, he asked himself—he wrenched her up from a prone position, holding her clothes balled in his left fist, looking at her. She got to her feet and ran. Frost hunkered down behind the deadfall, both M-16s in his fists, waiting.

He could hear running noises, shouts. There was a shot. There were more shouts, the words so fast and guttural he couldn't understand the Spanish.

But he could hear the movement, coming his way.

The one-eyed man waited.

He heard a curse, someone smashing into the half-rotted tree, then heard the footfalls along the ground, saw the first of the men jump the deadfall, then the next man and the next. He stopped counting after they reached nine, and then there were no more.

Frost pushed himself up to his knees, bracing the M-16s against his hip bones, opening fire with both assault rifles at once, shouting, "Eat lead, you bas—" But his shout was drowned out in the roar of his gunfire. Some of the men just fell, some spun, some tried turning and shooting back. One of them got his weapon going, the log beside Frost pulverizing, termites and rotted wood spraying into the air.

Frost kept firing, the gun in his right hand out, the one in his left hand still going, then it was out as well.

He stood up, resting the rifles against the rotted log, the metal too hot to touch.

He heard the noise, started to wheel and fall at the same time, his right fist wrapping around the butt of the Metalifed High Power, snatching it from the leather, the hammer still up, the safety whipping off under his right thumb as the man—maybe a slower runner than the rest, maybe more afraid—Frost didn't know—as the man raised his AK-47 and fired, the log almost completely dissolving now, Frost squinting against the shower of debris as Frost fired the High Power, once, then once again.

The assault rifle fire stopped, the man just standing there, bright blotches of blood on his chest.

Frost thought the eyes looked surprised.

The man collapsed to the ground.

Frost stood up, burning his hands on the rifles as he accidentally contacted skin to metal.

He blew the debris and the termites clear of the weapons, shaking his slouch hat.

After a few minutes, Miranda walked out of the jungle, her face now almost as white as the dead.

"You killed them all—you—"

"Hope so," Frost murmured, reloading his High Power. "Hope so."

Chapter Thirteen

"We'll camp here," Frost announced, pointing to the edge of the stream bed.

"All right," the girl nodded. They had been into the mountains for nearly an hour and already there was relief from the jungle heat and the insects. Frost's head ached, his body ached and he could barely stand his smell. He wore the same clothes he'd worn all through the previous day and the previous night, and the same clothes he'd bathed in sweat in the running battle in the jungle.

Frost started down the gravel embankment toward the stream, saying, "Are there any lethal microorganisms I should know about?"

"No—the water should be clear. I don't know if I would drink it without a purification tablet, but—"

"All right for bathing?" the one-eyed man asked her reaching the water's edge and bending down, splashing some of it up into his face.

The coolness almost made him pass out—it was as if his skin had longed for it.

"Frost—Hank?"

Frost turned and looked at her, water dripping down past his eye, his eyepatch wet. He snorted water from his mustache. "What, Miranda?"

"You must sleep."

"Yes," and he turned back to the stream-bed, starting to strip away his shoulder harness and his shirt.

"Hank?"

"What Miranda?" he asked again.

"Hank—I want us to make love."

Frost sloshed his shirt into the water, squeezing it tight in his fists before answering her.

"All right, Miranda—I'd like that too."

"But after you sleep."

"Yes—but after I sleep," Frost answered. And after he bathed . . .

Frost opened his eye, almost feeling a chill, but the coolness of the mountain air still welcome to him. He pulled the sleeping bag up over his bare chest, against the cold, looking for Miranda. He saw her, sitting on a pile of rocks further up along the stream, her M-16 in her hands. Guarding him. He smiled at the thought. The one-eyed man took a Camel from the pack he had opened just before going to sleep. He lit it in the flame of his Zippo, glancing at his wristwatch simultaneously.

It would be dark in a few hours, he realized. And he had slept for six hours.

He could have used twelve, but six would keep him going.

He inhaled the smoke deep into his lungs, trying to awaken fully.

"Miranda," he called out.

She turned, standing up, facing him. "Si?"

"What you said before?"

"Si . . ."

"Come here," and Frost stubbed out the cigarette in the dirt beside his sleeping bag, then tossed the cigarette away.

She walked toward him, unbuttoning the front of her shirt. She set the rifle down against a rock, then pulled the shirt from her bush shorts, stripping it away completely. She wore the T-shirt she had worn earlier, and she pulled this off over her head, her dark hair catching up in it, then cascading to her shoulders—bare—as the T-shirt pulled away. She dropped it on top of her shirt, then dropped to her knees beside him in the sleeping bag where he watched her. "You do my pants," she murmured.

Frost nodded, reaching for the belt, undoing it, then the button and then the zipper. He pulled it down all the way, then placed his right hand inside the front of her panties, feeling the hair there, the moistness that was already there.

As he rubbed his fingers against her, he heard the moaning start, deep down in her chest it seemed, like a kitten purring, then the noise coming from her throat.

He looked at her face. Her eyes were closed, her head cocked back, and her eyelids fluttered as he moved his hand against her.

He stopped, helping her up so he could push her pants and her panties down, then opening the side of his sleeping bag, pulling her down beside him.

She had kicked off her boots—Frost smiled remembering the habit she had of keeping them unlaced. He wondered if this were the reason. He pulled the pants and the panties down, off her legs. All she wore were the knee socks she'd worn before. He didn't bother with them, his hands moving to her breasts, kneading them under his fingers, feeling her fingers exploring him as well. "Hank," she whispered.

"I'm here," he told her, slipping between her thighs.

"Hank . . ."

"I know," he told her, feeling her hands on him, feeling himself digging against her.

He shuddered for an instant, and so did she, her back arching as he placed his left hand under it, her abdomen close against his.

He bent his head, kissing the nipple of her left breast, then kissing her neck, then his mouth coming down on hers, feeling the saltiness there that he hadn't tasted, but was tasting now, feeling her tongue, the tip of it hot against his.

She was moving under him, and the one-eyed man whispered to her, "Time—we've got plenty of it. Relax," and the movement slowed, but became steadier and he felt her arms wrapping around him tight . . .

Frost pulled his shirt on, buttoning it—a clean one from his pack. He started tying his combat boots, watching Miranda Ceballos, on guard again. She was staring at something, up along the stream but out of sight to Frost because of a bend. He was tempted to call out to her, but he thought better of it, securing his last bootlace and reaching across to his pistol.

"No se mueva, Americano!"

99

Frost froze, hearing the ominous and familiar metallic click—a submachinegun bolt pulling into the open position.

"Mantengase cellado!"

Frost heard the command, but decided against it, shouting out, "Miranda—Miran—" reaching out for the Metalifed High Power, then feeling something crash down on the back of his neck. Frost fell forward, his eye flooded with crimson and gold floaters, a nauseous feeling in the pit of his stomach. He rolled over, and standing above him was a man, a submachinegun muzzle inches from Frost's face. "Despacio—parese."

Frost eyed the man, the submachinegun and the half dozen men, similarly armed, ringing him now. Frost obeyed, standing up, slowly. He looked behind him. He saw Miranda, similarly ringed.

"Vayase para alla," the man who'd spoken before snapped. "Sus manos arriba!"

Frost raised his hands, cursing under his breath, starting to walk slowly toward the ring of men surrounding Miranda. The ring opened, and he could see Miranda, her M-16 still in her right hand, a smile on her face. "Bitch," Frost murmured. It was the M-19 and Miranda had betrayed him.

About six feet from Miranda and the half dozen subgun armed M-19 personnel near her, Frost heard the voice from behind him. "Parese donde esta!" Frost stopped walking, turning around and looking at the man behind him with the subgun, the one giving the orders. "No se mueva," the man snapped. Frost didn't move.

"Que passa?" Frost asked.

"Silencio!"

Frost shut up, watching the twelve subguns, all aimed at him, then looking at Miranda. She was laughing. Then she spoke. "Hank—Hank. Stupido. Baje sus pantalones—sus pantalones!"

"Bullshit, lady!" Frost rasped.

Then he felt the muzzle of the subgun against the side of his head. "You better kill me right now, because if I get out of this, you've had—"

"Sus pantallones!"

Frost opened his belt, then the button and then unzipped his fly, letting his pants drop as he'd been told. There was laughter from the subgun-armed terrorists.

"Quitese toda su ropa," the one who had given the commands before snapped. He gestured with the subgun. Frost for an instant wished looks could kill—the man would have been dead. Frost took his hands down slowly, then started unbuttoning his shirt. He stripped it away and dropped it beside him, then slowly bent down to begin unlacing his combat boots, first the right, then the left. He pushed them off, looking at Miranda. "Toda," the subgunner laughed. Frost pulled off his pants and dropped them, then his socks. He wore only his underpants. "Toda su ropa," the man insisted, and Frost took off his underpants.

"Mireme!" Miranda commanded, and Frost looked at her. "Arrodillese en el suelo!"

Frost didn't move. She took the muzzle of the M-16 and pressed it to his forehead. "Arrodillese!" Frost dropped to his knees. "Ponga sus manos atras de usted!"

Frost put his hands behind him, watching her

face, seeing her nod to one of the men with the sub-gun. Then quickly, Frost could feel rope being bound around his wrists, his arms being pulled up behind him and the rope snaking around his neck. Then he could feel it being tied to his wrists again.

"Parese," she commanded, and Frost, awkwardly because his balance was off, got to his feet, standing there, naked, tied, in front of her. She walked closer to him and spat in his face.

Frost spit back, rasping, "Puta!"

She slapped his face, but the one-eyed man didn't move. If he'd known a word worse than "slut" he would have used it.

She said nothing, her face red, the muscles around her eyes tight. She pointed upstream and Frost looked where she pointed. There was a half dozen burros, all laden with packs.

"Vamonos," the one with the subgun who had spoken before rasped. Frost started walking, toward the burros, then stopped when the man shouted, "Alto." He heard something in Spanish too rapid for him to catch, but the next instant the men around him had picked him up and thrown him across the back of one of the burros. There was a noose of rope put around his neck and he could feel his ankles being tied as he hung across the back of the pack animal. He could barely move his head as he felt ropes going across his shoulders and legs, further securing him to the animal. But he could see Miranda Ceballos as she walked up beside him, the smile back on her face.

"I'm saving you," she said in English. "For Emilio."

Frost had heard the name, but only the first, never the last. He was reputedly the head of the terrorist activity for M-19.

His voice hoarse, his back aching, Frost rasped, "Thanks a lot."

The burro started moving and Frost started regretting eating an hour earlier.

Chapter Fourteen

When darkness came, they were still moving along the trail up into the mountains, and what few flies there were, Frost could feel sucking blood from his immobile body as the burro jogged lumberingly along. Each piece of brush was a new threat, the branches swatting at his face and shoulders and the soles of his feet as he moved. And the cold — he was shaking with it, his wrists and ankles already numb and the feeling gone, his legs and his arms racked with chills as was the rest of his body. He had tried moving once, to shift position, but the noose around his neck which secured his head by the base of the burro's midsection had only tightened and it had taken him five minutes to flex the muscles in his neck sufficiently to loosen it.

By what he gauged to be midnight, the pain in his back had taken over, travelling up into his neck and his head, and this, combined with being half upside down and the blood rushing to his head, soon had put him into a sea of agony. It was torture of the most subtle kind.

He could barely reckon time or distance, but as the sky began to grey and he assumed it to be near dawn, his kidneys could no longer hold up. He urinated, feeling the momentary warmth around his groin and his abdomen and the tops of his thighs, then afterward the cold. The thought crossed his mind, fleetingly, that he hoped the packs on the burro had contained something important to M-19—something he'd just urinated on . . .

Frost opened his eye, cold sun glaring down on him, and the burro had stopped. He could no longer raise his head, but he could see combat booted feet standing around the burro. He heard someone talking—Miranda? But he wasn't certain. The blood pounding in his head was making hearing difficult for him. Suddenly, he felt himself slipping—the ropes cut?—and he fell to the dirt beside the burro.

Hands rolled him over.

Miranda was standing over him, her rifle aimed at his head. He felt hands hauling him up to his feet, then the hands letting go. Frost fell forward, stiff, like a felled tree, tasting blood as he hit the dirt. His nose was stiff, aching and he thought he might have broken it. He had to breathe from his mouth. The hands were hauling him up again, to his feet, but this time they held him.

He couldn't hold up his head.

He felt a hand grab at his hair, snapping his head back, and he saw a face.

"I am Emilio Barranca. Miranda—she tells me you are a policeman. Were you sent here to arrest me? Or kill me, maybe?"

The face was long, overly long, the eyes sunken and dark, the cheeks hollow and when Barranca smiled, the teeth were yellow with nicotine.

"Have a hard journey, amigo," Barranca laughed, then Frost's head was jerked back even more, but by

105

someone else, because Frost could see both of Barranca's hands.

The right backhanded him across the face and Frost could feel the blood again as it spurted from his nose. Then the hammering started — against his midsection, and Frost tried doubling over with it, but the hand still held his head up by his hair. The pain kept coming, coming, and then it stopped or he couldn't feel any more.

The hands let go and Frost sank to the ground.

He opened his eye, seeing Miranda standing above him, then he saw her foot striking out toward his face . . .

Chapter Fifteen

Frost opened his eye and moved his head. His nose was stiff, and he couldn't breathe through it, and his lips were cracked and swollen. His tongue felt too big—it was dry. He coughed and smiled—the pain worsening when he did—but at least he hadn't coughed up blood.

Frost looked below him—then he realized. He looked above him. His hands were tied together, secured to some sort of wooden framework, and beneath him, his bound ankles swung at least a foot off the ground. He turned his head—he was suspended inside a wooden cage, like a tiger cage, only wider, about the size of a small bathroom, and the cage was inside a hut. The roof of the hut was comparatively high.

He looked beneath him and ahead—there was a guard in the hut, and no one else.

"Agua," Frost rasped hoarsely. "Agua."

The guard turned around, looked at him, then took a canteen off the table. The guard stood up and walked toward Frost's cage.

"Agua?"

"Si?" Frost gasped.

"Por favor?"

"Agua—por favor."

The man opened the canteen, then inverted it, letting the water run out onto the dirt floor. He laughed, dropping the canteen and walked away.

Frost watched the canteen as the water ran from it, his head sagging.

He remembered telling Lew that he didn't give up. He wondered if he was going to eat the words now.

And he wondered if he'd have the chance to kill Miranda Ceballos . . .

Frost opened his eye again. He realized he had passed out. There was another guard, a different man. On the dirt floor the canteen was still there, but all the water dribbled out now.

He forced himself to think. They would not just let him die—there would be torture, or some sort of ritual-like death for him. There was no feeling in his wrists and hands and little feeling left in his feet. It wouldn't be long before the flesh began to wither and gangrene took over—if it hadn't already.

Frost looked up, the door of the hut opening. Something stirred in him—the desire to live, at least a little while longer. It was Miranda Ceballos.

She walked over to the guard, the guard smiling at her, Miranda laughing. She had changed from the bush shorts she'd worn before, her hair down, a white blouse and a long skirt and a shawl across her shoulders replacing them. Under other circumstances, Frost thought, he would have called her beautiful.

"Capitan Frost—are you still alive?" she taunted, laughing.

Frost eyed her, unable to speak because of his thirst.

She pulled a knife from under the shawl, then said over her shoulder something Frost couldn't understand.

The guard stood up, walked over to the wooden cage and unlocked the chain closing it shut, then opened the door. Miranda Ceballos stepped inside.

She stood a few feet from Frost, smiling as she looked at him. Frost wished for the instant that he weren't so dehydrated.

"Emilio wants to talk with you—Capitan Frost," and she turned to the guard, telling him in Spanish to cut Frost down.

The guard nodded, leaving the cage and returning with a chair. Miranda handed him her knife. Frost started sucking in his breath—against the inevitable pain of falling and for the one chance he felt he might ever get.

"De un paso—"

"Si," Miranda nodded, stepping back toward the wall of the cage.

Frost could see the man's face, the smile as he reached up with the knife, to cut the rope holding Frost swinging from the top of the cage. The one-eyed man sucked in his breath hard, and as he felt himself start to drop, he wrenched his body hard to his left, against the man cutting him down, knocking the man from the chair and against the wooden bars, Frost's own body falling on top of the guard.

Miranda started to move, but Frost swept his bound-together ankles toward her, catching her right leg. Miranda stumbled, falling back against the bars.

The one-eyed man rolled himself over, seeing the knife. His hands were useless, his arms paining him so

109

badly he could not lower them fully. He used his feet to push himself closer to the knife, getting the wooden handle of the butcher knife into his teeth.

He rolled over, onto his belly, his neck arched to keep the knife blade clear of the ground. Miranda was starting to stir.

Frost swung his body around, to get his feet out toward her, trying to edge across the dirt, wrenching his body to keep it moving. He had himself turned around.

Miranda was starting to her feet and Frost arched his back, the pain agonizing to him as he snapped out his feet, catching Miranda on the side of the head, knocking her head back against the wooden bars.

She slumped, her eyes closing, and was still.

Frost sank down, the knife still in his teeth.

He tried moving his arms, the pain and the stiffness almost making him faint. He tried again, this time getting his arms down far enough that by bending forward, he could just barely touch the tip of the butcher knife blade to the ropes. His hands were purple, and his fingers couldn't move. He began to cut, working the knife by moving his head side to side and up and down.

He had no idea how long it took him, but he broke through one of the ropes.

Frost leaned back, his head against the wooden bars. The man who'd cut him down was beginning to stir. Frost tried to pull at the ropes, his hands not responding, then he tried again. Slowly, agonizingly, the rope burning against his flesh, he ripped his hands free. The pain almost made him pass out.

His hands still wouldn't work, but he dropped the

knife from his mouth, his arms able to move, but painfully and slowly.

He swept his arms toward the knife, getting the handle between his wrists, then by squeezing his hands together, getting the knife up. He pushed himself away from the bars, half falling, the knife between his wrists gouging into the throat of the stirring man beside the bars less than a yard from him. There was a choking sound as blood spurted across Frost's naked chest and his face.

Frost rolled away, the knife in the man's throat still. His hands weren't strong enough to extract it.

Frost began moving his arms, slowly, trying to flex his fingers. He couldn't.

He moved his hands along his naked thighs, rubbing the stiff fingers against them to try to bring back circulation and feeling.

The second finger of his right hand began to tingle . . .

Someone should have been coming, Frost knew—had it been ten minutes, had it been an hour? He didn't know, all time gone to him but his hands finally able to move. There were gouge lines along his wrists, and in some places the skin was torn or burned away from the ropes, but his hands were starting to work.

He reached out with his right hand, slowly, his arms aching from the muscle strain.

Slowly, clumsily, his fingers wrapped around the handle of the knife and then the one-eyed man wrenched it free.

And in the man's trouser belt was a revolver. Frost dropped the knife for a moment, then pulled out the gun. It was an old, large framed Colt Official Police .38, the bluing worn, but the gun clean looking and serviceable-seeming. Slowly, not trusting his coordination yet to pick up something so small as a cartridge, he opened the cylinder. The gun was fully loaded. He closed the cylinder, feeling a smile crossing his lips.

Frost picked up the knife—awkwardly but securely—and began to cut the ropes binding his ankles.

He was free. He inhaled hard, flexing his legs, debating if he should attempt to stand.

He grasped the wooden bar nearest him and tried to pull himself up. He couldn't get past his knees yet.

On his knees then, he crawled across the dirt to the dead guard, undressing him—he needed the clothes.

Frost left the underwear, and the shoes were impossibly small, but the shirt, despite the soaked-through blood, fit well enough. Frost didn't bother buttoning it. He pulled on the pants, buttoning the fly and securing the wide belt around his waist.

In the trouser pocket were a dozen rounds of .38 Special ammo, only 158 grain round nosed lead, but better than nothing he realized.

He tried again to stand, this time rising to his full height and leaning against the bars.

"Miranda," and he raised the pistol as she opened her eyes.

"Hank!" she gasped.

"Miranda," he repeated, still barely able to talk, but the thirst he had for water less than the thirst he had for her life.

"Thank God—but I would have helped you. Here," and she started to get unsteadily to her feet.

Frost levelled the gun at her. "No—Hank—please.

That is why I came. Barranca didn't want to talk to you. I was here to help you escape."

Frost wanted to scream at her, or to shoot her.

"Water—let me get you water—please," and she started to edge through the open door of the wooden cage. Frost sank down to his knees against the bars, too tired to stand, but levelling the revolver at her still. He watched her across the front sight.

"Please Hank—por favor." She started bringing a canteen toward him. Frost waited until she was near him, then dropped to her knees beside him. He reached out his left hand, taking the canteen, then gulped water from it, choking, throwing up the water across the front of his shirt, sagging back against the bars, barely able to breathe.

"More slowly—please," and she took the canteen from his left hand and held it in her hands, bringing it up to his lips. "Here," and she held it for him as he drank.

Frost cocked the revolver, and she edged back. "No—Hank. There was no other way. They had us—I could only tell them that I worked with them, that you were a policeman. That was the only way they would not have killed us both. Please—Madre de Dios—you must believe me."

Frost took the canteen from her and drank, realizing he wanted to urinate now very badly. He told himself it was psychological. "Your clothes and your weapons—they are in that chest there. You can be free, to escape into the trees, to wait and then kill Barranca. That is why you came, no?"

Frost said nothing, not even knowing if he could.

"You are here to assassinate him—that is why you

113

have come. I know. And I want to help you. That is why I came here, now, to set you free. But you must hurry—how long has it been?'"

"I—don't—don't," and he gave up.

"You don't know. But I will be missed. You must hurry. I can bring you food, tomorrow morning. There is a pool above the camp, a place where I go to bathe. No one follows me there."

"Why?"

"I will tell the truth—I am Emilio Barranca's woman. They would not dare."

Frost licked his lips. They were cracked still and swollen-feeling, and he could barely breathe through his nose. "I'm gonna kill you—right now," he told her, raising the still-cocked revolver and pointing it at her head.

"Think! If Barranca had wanted to question you further, he would have been here by now, looking for me, looking for the guard. Think! You must see it—I came to free you. I would have stabbed the guard—with this," and she picked up the butcher knife, "but he needed it to cut you down. Think!"

"Kiss off, lady," and Frost started to squeeze the trigger.

"Wait—please! I am a policeman, like you. Please—trust me one more time. Why do I not scream?"

Frost eased the pressure against the trigger. "Because of this."

"And if you shoot me, then what? Barranca and his men will come. You will die—but I can help you escape. As I had planned to do. Please—trust me. There was no other way."

Frost lowered the hammer on the revolver. "Help me up," he ordered.

She reached down to him, touching him slowly at first near the shoulders. He kept the revolver pointed at her.

He got to his feet, unsteadily. "You can escape."

"I can't walk too well," Frost murmured. "So I can't escape too well."

"You must—I will aid you. Come."

"My gear," Frost told her.

"Si—I will get it."

He looked at his left wrist. "My watch—where is it?"

"The guard—I think—"

Frost looked down at the man he had killed, for the first time really noticing him. There was no watch. "No—the other one—the one who was here before. He took it."

"Where is he?"

"He will be coming back—any time now, to replace this one."

"We'll wait," Frost snapped. "Help me walk while we do—now," and Frost leaned heavily against her, his left arm on her shoulders and they started to walk.

The time wore on, Frost trying to keep track of it but still not one hundred percent functional yet. They would stop every moment or so and he would peer out the crack in the doorway, keeping the gun against Miranda's head as he did to ensure her silence. Finally, he saw someone coming across the darkened compound. It would be the guard.

He looked at Miranda. "Take the butcher knife—and when he comes in, kill him—or I'll kill you both," Frost told her flatly.

She looked at him a moment, her eyes wide with what Frost supposed to be terror. "Si," and she ran back across the hut to the cage, picking up the butcher knife.

Frost cocked the revolver, needlessly he knew, but he distrusted what the double action pull might be like. He waited beside the doorway into the hut, Miranda on the other side.

The guard stepped through.

Frost pointed the revolver as the man went for his assault rifle.

Then the man's eyes almost popped from his head and he crumpled forward, the knife sticking out of his back between the shoulder blades to the right of the spine.

Frost looked at Miranda, saying slowly, "I'll regret this—I still think you're a liar, but I'll let you live. At least for now."

He looked down at the dead man's left wrist. "Now get me my watch—quick." Miranda knelt for the watch and Frost cracked the butt of the revolver down behind her right ear . . .

Chapter Sixteen

Frost sat in the icy-cold stream water, the water splashing over him, the old Colt revolver on a rock beside him, covered with spray and droplets of water visible to him in the moonlight.

He had taken soap from his pack and bathed, several times, in the mountain stream, because he had been unable to live with himself the way he had been. And the old revolver was beside him because he had not wanted to expose his own gun or ammunition to the water, despite the Metalife finished pistol's rust resistance.

He was naked again, except for his Rolex, and he had washed that as well. His hands still trembled, but the fingers worked and he had decided there would be no permanent damage.

After cold-cocking Miranda, he had taken his gear and left the camp, slowly, making his way into the trees and then up along the sides of the encampment. It was like an Apache stronghold from the American southwest of the last century, he thought, thinking back to it. Rocks on each side, rising high into the mountains. Only one way in, but likely a secret way out. Guards everywhere. Frost had knifed three men in leaving.

He had rationalized knocking out Miranda. If she

were a liar, as he thought, she would scream the moment he left, or shoot at him herself. If she were sincere, then the knock on her head would make it appear she had discovered him escaping and he had tried to kill her but not succeeded. He would meet her at the mountain pool, that he had already determined. If it were a set-up, he would stay far enough away. If it weren't she would be there regardless.

Frost looked at the luminous black face of the Rolex. It had survived unscathed. And it was midnight. He would have to awaken with the dawn, or otherwise miss Miranda, if indeed she came.

Frost stepped up out of the water, looking down at his body in the moonlight. The scars would heal—again, he told himself. They always did.

He dried off, still feeling cold from the water, and began to dress—his last change of fresh clothes.

Finally, he slipped the Cobra Comvest over his cammie shirt—he had no intention of removing it until he was out of Colombia, it and the High Power he carried there.

He started looking among the rocks as he sat tying his combat boots. He needed a place to stay until morning.

And he found himself smiling—he'd been right so far in what he'd told Lew—just never give up.

Chapter Seventeen

Frost opened his eye, sunlight streaming down on him where he lay among the rocks. His clothes were damp from the moisture of the night air, and his legs and arms were stiff, as was his back.

He looked around, seeing no one—yet. He started to stand up, then heard something, a shout in guttural Spanish.

Taking the binoculars, he focused the right tube down below him, toward the stream. Three men, all armed with AK-47s. A search party. He wondered for an instant: even if Miranda were sincere, would Barranca allow her to go to her pool for her bath—with the dangerous American still at large?

Frost scanned the rest of the area below him. Jagged rock outcroppings, some scattered foliage and—no other men.

Frost had done the thing he'd felt Barranca would feel least likely. Rather than start down and away from the camp, toward the jungle, he had elected to head up higher, into the mountains. It was likely, then, Frost decided, that Miranda had been telling him the truth—at least partially. Because if a clandestine meeting with her at the pool above the camp were something Barranca knew about, there would have been more searchers. But apparently, there were not.

The reasoning wouldn't lull him into total trust, he told himself. It was possible Barranca was second-guessing him better than he imagined. That Miranda had lied—again. Send out only a few searchers, enough to make it appear legitimate, then wait for the American at the pool when he comes to see Miranda. Frost smiled at the thought—whatever he believed, he had to see her.

He caught up his slouch hat and started down out of the rocks. The pool—he had gone there the previous night, before his stream-bath—was a half mile away. It would take time getting there slowly. Either that or kill the three searchers below him.

He waited in the rocks a while longer, thinking. Guns were out of the guestion, but there was his little Gerber knife, there was his bayonet—and his hands. They still shook, but not as much as the previous night—and they could kill.

He mentally and physically shrugged, then started down from the rocks. He could intercept the three M-19 searchers along the natural path they would follow among the rocks, up higher into the mountains.

He would do that . . .

Frost waited, hidden behind an outcropping of rocks, above the trail, the trail some eight feet or so below his position. His M-16 was with his pack, safely out of sight. The bayonet, the longer of his two-edged weapons, was in his right fist. He waited.

After ten minutes by the watch on his wrist, he heard them, one of them talking something about when they caught the American this time they would cut out his other eye. Frost smiled. They wouldn't have the chance.

He waited.

The talking was louder now, and laughter, more about what they would do to the American. How Barranca wanted the American for striking his woman.

Frost liked the ring of that—it lent credence to Miranda's story.

He waited. Beneath him now, he could see the first of them, holding his AK-47 more like a broom than a rifle, almost dragging the muzzle along the rocky ground. Then the next man, and then the third, all three walking in file along the trail, talking, looking up into the rocks occasionally.

But terrorists weren't usually exceedingly bright, he thought—except for the leader.

The third man was directly under him now and Frost jumped.

His knees impacted midway along the terrorist's back, Frost's knife driving down into the carotid artery and ripping flesh and the clothing covering it as the man fell forward and Frost slipped to the ground.

The second man was turning around and Frost went for him, ramming the bayonet in low, below the belt, into the crotch. The first man was turning, already raising his AK-47 to fire. Too late to stop him, Frost shoved the body of the second terrorist against the muzzle of the rifle. The bullets ripped through the flesh as Frost rolled away.

Frost had lost the bayonet, still in the gut of the second terrorist, but had his other knife, and hurled himself onto the back of the third terrorist, hammering the blade down into the neck, again and again until the writhing of the man under him ceased.

Frost pushed himself up.

The first man was dead, and so was the third man, but

the second terrorist wasn't dead yet despite the bayonet sticking out of his crotch and the bullet holes in his back. Frost fixed that—and the second terrorist died . . .

The one-eyed man stuck to the higher ground, the going more slow there, but his view of the terrain and the tactical plot it would present if he saw any more of the M-19 terrorists making it the safer bet.

And already, the pool was in sight . . .

Frost crept up through the rocks, not knowing if it was a trap or not. There was a woman in the pool, bathing herself, the water only covering her below the waist, her breasts sudsy with the soap she used, the water clouded around her. And there was another woman—this one fully dressed, perhaps about thirty, Frost judged, and an M-16 in her hands, guarding the first woman. Frost assumed the rifle belonged to Miranda.

Frost crouched down in the rocks, thinking. Miranda would not have been so obvious as to have a guard in plain sight—and a woman, like herself? He tried to structure a scenario. Barranca would have forbidden that she go alone to take the bath, then compromised with her by sending another woman, one who could handle a gun. It had been clear from the borrowed clothes he'd taken from the dead guard in the hut the previous night that cleanliness was not something with which the M-19 had an overriding concern.

Frost looked back toward the pool. The woman with the M-16 had a pistol belt around her waist, but not Miranda's. Miranda's pistol belt was near her clothes—Frost could see them hung on a tree limb near the water.

The woman guard, like Barranca, like all the others, was herself an M-19 terr.

Frost debated what to do. If he killed the woman, perhaps a story could be contrived. He wondered. If he only knocked her unconscious, then . . . The one-eyed man smiled, an idea coming to him.

His old friend Ron Mahovsky was good at the technique, better than he was. You focused concentration on something else, other than the man—or in this case, woman—that you stalked. The idea was that the other person might somehow get a mental vibration that he was a target, the sixth sense rearing and alerting him. Frost didn't argue with the idea of a sixth sense—it had saved his life many times—too many, he thought. He was less than twenty yards away from the woman terrorist.

Hands only, he told himself—otherwise she could be killed.

He crept on, concentrating on everything from Beethoven to Hungarian food, trying to keep his mind off—He stopped again, ten yards from her.

"Now," he murmured to himself, trying to force concentration on Miranda instead—naked there in the pool, lovely, and even partially trustworthy it seemed. Five yards and the woman terrorist was turning around, raising her M-16. Frost jumped toward her, half wheeling, his right foot snaking up, the sore muscles of his leg screaming at him not to move like that. His foot connected with her jaw, once, twice, and the woman's head snapped back and she collapsed backwards, her face into the water of the pool.

Frost reached down, pulling her up before she drowned, starting to take her pistol as he heard Miranda saying, "That was a good kick. Martial arts?"

"Tae Kwan Do—I think," Frost smiled.

He had the woman's pistol now and the M-16, and he snatched up Miranda's pistol belt. "You came," she said, starting out of the water.

"Stay in the water—just get all scrubby clean while we talk."

"I want to get dressed."

"Ask again and I'll cut your clothes to pieces with a knife. We talk before I trust you any further."

"What about Juanita?"

"Her?" and Frost gestured to the unconscious female terrorist at his feet as he bent to tie and gag her. "She'll have a sore jaw—maybe some bad teeth—probably weren't too good to start out with. But she'll live.

"But she'll—"

"No, she won't—I figured that out already."

"When can I get out of the water," Miranda insisted.

"After you tell me what the hell is goin' on—so start," and Frost sat down on a rock beside the pond, feeling for all the world stupid, talking to a woman taking a bath and holding a gun on her nonetheless. But he did both—talked with her and never moved the muzzle of his M-16.

Miranda reiterated what she had told him the previous night—that she was a policeman just as she had claimed. Frost laughed when she used the word—looking at her naked there in the water, she was definitely not a policeman. She insisted that as Barranca's woman for the past eighteen months she had learned everything she could about M-19 in preparation for smashing at least this cell, for getting

Barranca. She had thought at first that Frost's appearance on the scene would spoil that, but then, after seeing how fiercely he had fought when they were in the camp of the villagers who liked to murder their guests, formulated a different plan. For that reason she had decided that under any circumstances, he had to stay alive. "I could not let you be harmed."

"Aww no," Frost sneered. "What do you call being packed up into the mountains stark naked on the back of a burro, then beaten up by Barranca, then hung up in that cage—I'm lucky I didn't lose both hands."

"That was just it—it was a risk. I knew that. I assumed you were just playing it to the hilt back when they caught us—I didn't know you would actually be so silly as to interpret my actions as those of a traitor."

"Yeah—silly of me, wasn't it."

"But—"

"Remember kicking me in the head after Barranca pounded lumps on me."

"If I hadn't, he would have done worse . . . It was a calculated risk."

"But nobody asked me to help calculate," Frost told her. "Why the naked routine?"

"I felt that the more helpless I made you appear the greater chance they would not kill you immediately when we arrived at the camp. It was all for your own good—to accomplish your mission."

"And just what is my mission, lady—what? Kill Barranca?"

"Is it not?"

Frost shrugged. "Yeah—it is. How'd you know?"

"For what other reason could you have come here, have wanted to come here? It was the only reason. And I will help you now to do it."

"And how's that," Frost asked her.

"First—I am clean now—I want to get out of the water."

"Okay, get out of the water," Frost told her, standing up and taking a few steps back. She started out of the water then, beautiful, naked, wet, shivering. She reached for her towel and Frost watched as she dried herself. She reached then for her blouse and Frost told her, "I didn't say anything about getting dressed."

"You wish to humiliate me—like I humiliated you—I know this. Are you going to beat me?"

"What if I were," Frost asked her.

"You would have the right."

He knew in his heart he was being conned, but for the moment he didn't care.

Frost lowered the muzzle of the assault rifle, looking at her—"You're a pretty woman, Miranda—at least on the outside," and she came into his arms, her mouth searching up for his. "Miranda," he whispered, touching his lips to her ear.

"You will have to hit me—later. So it will look authentic, like last night. I still have the bump—here," and she moved her face so her right ear was near his mouth. He kissed her ear, and she turned her face up to him, smiling. "I think I love you a little, Hank."

Frost kissed her mouth hard—then thought how stupid he was. But he kept on kissing her . . .

They found a place upstream of the pool, a place where if the woman terrorist awoke, she couldn't see them. They spread her skirt on the ground, under her, and Frost lay down on top of her, her nipples rising, erect under his touch, her loins seeming almost to quiver when he touched her. Her eyes, her face—he wondered if it were her beauty, or the chance that he might never get out of the Andes alive, or perhaps just the danger of making love to someone whom you didn't trust.

It struck the one-eyed man as bizarre—love and trust seemed to be virtually synonymous, yet here he was, contradicting the parallels—for he didn't trust her, but what they did felt good to him.

As he slipped between her thighs, she moaned for him, called him lover, and he wondered, was she lying even then?

Her body raised up under him, fusing with his it seemed, and there was a wildness about her, a frenzy, as if she not only expected to please and be pleased, but demanded it.

And once when Frost realized he had caused her pain inadvertently, it seemed to him as though she enjoyed it. He did not understand her, her mind. But he could understand her body, its desires, its demands. Her lips were full, moist, almost seeming to draw him into her as he kissed her. "Miranda," he whispered once, the name almost hypnotic . . .

Chapter Eighteen

"Miranda," Frost whispered, alone, the woman gone. He shook his head, lighting a cigarette, a smile crossing his lips. "Miranda . . ."

Frost studied the crude map she had drawn him, after they had made love, after—He put down the map, inhaling hard on his cigarette.

She was fascinating, he realized, because of the fact that she was so unalterably deceitful—and for a moment Frost felt insane for having made love to her—was it all a cheat, a fraud, every sigh, every moan of passion? Was it really loathing, an act to be carried out for his benefit?

Frost studied the glowing tip of his cigarette, wondering—Was it perhaps all an act for her own benefit? Masturbatory?

He inhaled the smoke again, into his lungs. It was likely he would never see her again, except perhaps at a distance in—he checked his watch—three hours or so, and then never at all. He exhaled the smoke hard, wondering. "Miranda," he murmured . . .

The one-eyed man walked toward the high mountain plain that served as the M-19 airfield, where the pickup would be. Frost and Miranda had waited until the woman guard had started to stir, her bonds purposely loose enough that within a few minutes she would be free, but her weapons gone so she could not act. And her stirring was the cue for Frost and Miranda to begin the act—arguing, Frost calling Miranda every filthy name he could think of—all boiling down to traitor. Then striking at her, Miranda grabbing a gun, shooting at him and Frost pulling off into the rocks like a wounded animal. He had hidden there, waiting to see if it had been believed. Miranda sobbed hysterically on the ground as the female terrorist freed herself of the ropes on her wrists and ankles and pulled away the gag, then ran to Miranda. With Miranda's rifle, the female terrorist had run into the rocks, to look for him, but he had remained hidden. After a time, consoling Miranda, the female terrorist had walked off with her. Frost had watched after them for a time, then sat there in the rocks, lighting his cigarette and thinking. And as he walked now, he was no closer to understanding Miranda Ceballos than he had been. They had talked for a time, between the lovemaking and the playacting. Of many things.

Miranda's father had been a police officer, but a police officer because of a sense of social duty rather than the need for money. The family had always been independently wealthy. She had attended a university in the United States, studied police science there as well as the usual subjects, and then returned to Colombia. Six months after the murder of her father, she had joined the police force and been with it ever since, rising to her position of trust in the anti-terrorist/anti-smuggling campaign. She had never married, never feeling that her job afforded her the right to.

Frost could feel for the remark—that was his basic problem with Bess. He loved her, and she loved him, but to be married and continue his work seemed all but impossible at times, but then the thoughts of Bess would come back to him and he tried to attain the impossible. He wondered if he ever would.

And then Miranda had told him her plan. One of the smugglers who had handled the shipments of explosives to Miami for the pro-Castro terrorists there would be flying in that afternoon, flying in to pick up a load of cocaine, some marijuana and more of the explosives. She—Miranda—would be there, along with Emilio Barranca and some of his men. That would be Frost's chance, to kill Barranca.

She had asked Frost if he could fly an airplane. He had told her only in one direction—straight down. She had told him then he would have to improvise his escape. For if he failed in killing Barranca and Barranca apprehended him, Frost would wish himself dead many times before death actually came. And, if he killed Barranca, she would have to kill him. Because she was not only Barranca's woman, but they thought of her as second in command. And with Barranca dead, she would command the terrorist arm of M-19 and finally be in a position to destroy it from within.

Frost had wondered then as he wondered now—how much of it had been truth, and how much had been a lie? Had she been using him all along, to kill Barranca?

He mentally shrugged as he stopped on the lip of ground above the airfield, looking down on it. He had come to kill Barranca, and now he would do that. He looked at the M-16 in his hands. There were far better rifles for long distancing someone—far better, but the

M-16 would have to do. At the range, head and upper torso shots would be the only option, and several shots to make sure the deed was done properly.

Escape? He asked himself about that. And always the answer was the same—doubtful.

Frost studied the field, his glasses really unnecessary at the distance. It was a dirt track, apparently cleared by hand because of its unevenness. He doubted anything but the smallest of twin engines could have landed there. Grass of a sparse, brown color overgrew the field, and Frost didn't envy the pilot making the landing—potholes would likely be . . . He stopped, taking the Bushnells from his case and focusing through the right tube to stare at the center of the field.

A friend of his who had been a United States Marine had told him a trick Marine Corps sniper trainees often played on visiting dignitaries. "Hmm," the one-eyed man smiled.

He checked the Rolex on his wrist. There was time if he hurried, and the bayonet would do for the job, "Hmm," he murmured again. Then he started down toward the airfield, realizing now how he might escape . . .

"So much for clean clothes," he whispered to himself, watching as the Jeep carrying Miranda and Emilio Barranca arrived, two other Jeeps with it and a dozen men walking around the Jeeps, all armed with AK-47s. Barranca was less than a hundred yards away. Frost looked at his watch, lighting the Zippo in order to see it. It was dark where he hid, but not dark enough to make the luminous face legible. The plane was about due. Then, almost as if on cue, he could hear it, the drone of a single-engine plane.

Frost tucked down, waiting. When the plane landed . . . He checked the selector on the M-16 in his dirt-smudged hands—it was on full auto. Just a touch of the trigger and Barranca would be dead—he hoped.

The drone of the aircraft engine grew louder and Frost resisted the impulse to peek out and see it. He waited instead, once looking at Barranca and Miranda, Barranca's arm around her, Miranda smiling up at him, letting Barranca's other hand fondle her right breast as they stood together.

Frost asked himself, "Did she make love to me to make me jealous of Barranca—to give me the added push to—" He didn't finish the thought, but then of course subconsciously did. "To pull the trigger?" Frost waited, the aircraft engine loud now, almost directly above him.

Then the engine noise slowed and he imagined the plane taxiing. He looked out at Emilio Barranca again. At the edge of his peripheral vision, Frost could just see the plane. And now he could see two men climbing down from it. The one was blonde-haired, wore blue jeans and a knit shirt with a little reptile over the heart. A good target, Frost thought.

The other was Latin, decidedly so, dark-haired and dark-eyed, handsome. "Cuban?" Frost asked himself. Or perhaps a Colombian.

From what Frost could see of the plane, it seemed somehow different. He imagined what the difference might be. The rear seats, if any, gone, and the entire tail section given over to extra fuel and cargo capacity. Even now, some of the M-19 men were refueling the craft. It was a long hop from Colombia to Miami. Frost waited, watching as a wooden crate was loaded aboard by Emilio Barranca's men, then what looked like a bale of hay, then another, but these wrapped in what looked like canvas from the distance. Then Barranca personally handed the American a canvas musette bag. The American opened it and extracted a plastic bag, a white substance in it. The American opened the bag, touched his fingers into the bag, then to his lips.

The man spat, twice, then looked at Barranca and said something Frost could not hear, Barranca clapping him on the shoulder and smiling.

"Cocaine," Frost murmured. Drug identification was not one of his fields of expertise he realized, but coke seemed a safe bet.

The American handed Barranca an envelope and Barranca looked inside, said something and stuffed the envelope down inside his fatigue blouse. Miranda shook hands with the American—warmly—and the American said something to the Latin—the pilot? Frost hoped so.

First the Latin, then the American started back toward the plane, Barranca standing there, watching.

Frost inhaled, exhaled, then inhaled again, trying to even his nerves as well as his breathing.

The one-eyed man stood up, the dirt and dead grass and branches falling from his shoulders toward the shallow pit in which he had been camouflaged, and at the top of his voice, Frost shouted, "Barranca—guess who?"

As Barranca started to turn, Frost pumped the M-16's trigger, Miranda diving away, Barranca's chest and neck seeming to erupt in tiny explosions of blood. Frost kept firing, a ragged line of red holes starting along

Barranca's face and up into his forehead, then the red so dominant that the face itself was lost.

Frost fired out the M-16 toward the rest of Barranca's men and started to run, the branches and dirt that had covered his clothes and his hat falling, the plane already starting to taxi away, just as the one-eyed man had hoped it would.

Frost dumped the spent magazine from his rifle, letting it fall, ramming in the fresh one stuffed in his belt, then turning the rifle as he worked the bolt, firing as he ran, firing toward Barranca's men, running toward the taxiing aircraft.

The plane was taxiing past and Frost started to jump for it, then remembered the promise he had made to Miranda. He wheeled, shouldered the M-16 and flicked the selector to semi-auto. He fired once, Miranda grasping for her left shoulder as she spun away and fell against the Jeep she and Barranca had ridden.

If he owed her an obligation, he had fulfilled it, wounding her to help her story.

The one-eyed man wheeled again, shifting the selector back to full auto, the aircraft parallel with him, nearly out of his range.

Firing a fast burst, emptying the magazine of the M-16 he dropped the rifle to the ground, his hands flat out at his sides, running. His arms and legs ached, even the muscles in his chest pained him as he ran, the aircraft accelerating into the wind.

The prop draft washed him now as he ran beside the plane, his slouch hat blowing off, his right eye squinted against the dust and debris in the wash of air.

He bent lower into the run, throwing his arms back, charging toward the aircraft.

He dove, his hands grasping at one of the supports of the wing stem as the plane started up into the air, then bounced. The added weight of his body—he realized—had thrown it out of trim.

Ahead of them was the edge of the airfield and beyond this a sheer drop of perhaps three hundred feet. The pilot would be committed, would have to take off. Frost tried to pull himself up, onto the wing stem, his right hand groping, his left foot finding a purchase on the support as the plane started to climb.

Frost threw himself up, across the wing stem, the aircraft shuddering under him, the plane passing the edge of the field and starting to dip downward. Frost could see inside the cabin now, see the pilot wrestling the controls. Frost didn't envy the man.

Frost reached out for the door handle of the starboard side, trying to twist it open. But suddenly it swung wide, and the American was leaning out onto the wing stem a pistol in his left fist.

The American fired once, Frost falling across the wing stem, then the one-eyed man reaching up with his right hand, grasping for the gunhand. Frost had it, the automatic pistol discharging, Frost's fingers feeling the bite as the metal of the slide tore against his flesh.

"Damn you!" Frost shouted into the wind, still holding onto the gunhand, then throwing his own weight away from the fuselage, the American flying past him into the open, screaming, but the scream lost as the man hurtled over the edge of the wing and downward.

Frost felt himself slipping.

His right hand, bleeding, grasped the edge of the door frame. He could see the pilot, fighting the controls and at the same time trying to fumble the slide of a pistol.

Frost released the grip on the edge of the wing that he held with his left hand, throwing the hand up alongside the right, his legs now swinging free of the wing, in mid-air, the plane's engine sounding as though it was stalling.

The pilot was banking, the plane passing over the field. Frost glanced down once, hearing the faint echo of gunshots. Below, the three Jeeps were speeding across the field, almost directly under him.

Gunmen ringed the field, firing their automatic weapons skyward.

Frost couldn't see the reasoning of the pilot — because the man was going to try to land.

Frost wrenched himself up, his right leg having a purchase now. Frost sucked in his breath hard and threw himself forward, releasing his grip on the door frame and grabbing for the passenger seat.

He had it, the seatbelt wrapped around his left fist. Frost started to pull himself in, but the pilot was turning around, the pistol in his left hand hammering down toward Frost's right hand. Frost rolled right, almost losing the grip with his left hand on the seatbelt, but grabbing the tiny Gerber knife from the small of his back.

He rolled back left, the pistol hammering down again. Frost's right hand snaked out with the little knife, driving downward into the back of the hand of the pilot, pinning it by the fleshy portion beside the thumb knuckle to the seat.

Frost loosed the knife as the pilot screamed. The one-eyed man pulled himself up, falling against the plane seat, wrenching his knife free of the pilot's hand, throwing the automatic pistol out of the plane, then pulling the door closed.

The pilot's hand was bleeding, badly but not too badly, Frost quickly assessed.

The one-eyed man ripped his pistol from the leather, dropping the safety and pointing it at the pilot. At the same time, Frost handed the man the bandanna handkerchief from his pocket. "Here—don't bleed to death."

"I'm landing this—"

"Then I'm using this," Frost rasped. "You wanted to pass across the damned field before—well—go ahead," Frost snarled, eyeing the Uzi submachinegun in the corner.

"What?"

"Make a damned pass—one'll do it."

Frost gestured with the gun.

"Can you fly this thing?"

"No—but I can shoot this thing—real good," Frost told him.

"I can crash this!"

"And then you'll die anyway—fly me back to Florida and I'll get you off—at least a little."

The pilot looked at Frost, saying, "Cuba—I'll take you—"

"An aircraft crash would be preferable to the Cuban authorities for me—what's it gonna be?"

The pilot looked at him, Frost feeling the craft levelling off. "Florida."

"Good—make that pass," and Frost reached for the Uzi. There was a full thirty-two round magazine in it, and Frost didn't see any spares. He shrugged, working the bolt open with his bloodied right hand, the High Power in his left fist, still levelled at the pilot.

"They're shooting at us from down there," the pilot shouted.

"That's okay—just one fast pass'll do it." Frost pried open the passenger or co-pilot side storm window, getting the muzzle of the Uzi out. He knew his targets already. The men would be too small for the altitude. They were moving, the plane was moving. But the Jeeps. He remembered that all of them had carried spare gas cannisters.

"Make the pass."

"Beginning now," the pilot answered.

Frost rasped, "And remember, you try anything, the pistol is still in my left hand—at this range—"

"Yeah," the pilot snapped.

The one-eyed man smiled—he was beginning to like the guy.

The plane started down, low across the field, the men on the field noticing it, the Jeeps starting to move again.

Frost could see Miranda, huddled by the edge of the field, the woman—or at least some woman—terrorist beside her.

Frost started firing, pumping the trigger of the Uzi, the brass flying past his face and spraying the cockpit, the muzzle steadied in the niche of the storm window. He nailed the nearest Jeep as they passed toward it, the rear end of the Jeep erupting in flames, burning bodies of the M-19 terrorists sailing skyward as the vehicle exploded in a massive orange and black fireball. Frost took aim on the second Jeep, firing, the Jeep shuddering to a stop as the plane passed over it, the shadow of the aircraft barely clear of it as the Jeep exploded. Frost tried firing at the third Jeep, but the Uzi came up empty after a two round burst.

Frost looked at the pilot, smiling as he pulled the Uzi back inside. "Can't win 'em all!"

Chapter Nineteen

The radio link had been hard to establish, but as they had crossed over a Coast Guard Cutter in the Gulf, Frost had finally made contact. He had watched the Latin pilot, the man's face sweating as Frost had contacted the Coast Guard, telling what his cargo was and asking to be put in touch with Florida Department of Law Enforcement, namely with Lew Wilson.

A fighter from the naval base was dogging them as the link finally came on.

"Calling Cessna Golf Hotel X-Ray eight-one-niner, Calling—"

"Cessna Golf Hotel X-Ray eight-one-niner, reading you—over."

"Hank?"

Frost punched the push-to-talk button on the hand microphone. "Lew—bet you didn't think I was still alive."

"You're too damn dumb to know you're supposed to lie down—that's all. What the hell are you doin' comin' into Florida with a plane load of pot, coke and explosives, over?"

"Don't forget a pilot who tells me he's a Cuban national and doesn't have any papers and an Uzi submachinegun, over."

"What the hell is goin' on, Hank—over."

139

"Lew—gonna read you off some coordinates in a minute—this guy's primary landing field—probably buildin' it right now. Bring your guys—and be ready for bear. My little friend up here who's flyin' the plane—tells me because of the explosives should be a lot of heavily armed men down there. And just because you're so nice, I figured I'd invite you and all of your friends to the party." Frost read off the coordinates, then looked at the Cuban, then back at the microphone. "These guys play for keeps. Over."

"You come down in the middle of that—they could be—"

Frost punched the push-to-talk button several times to cut off Wilson. "I know, Lew—believe me. I know. Just be there on time. We'll be landing in roughly fifty-six minutes. Over."

"Fifty-six minutes! Over."

"Yeah—gives you time for a nap and everything. Over."

"Nap my—all right—but be careful—and stay near the radio. Wilson out."

"Out," Frost rasped, putting up the microphone. He looked at the Cuban, saying, "Mind if I smoke?"

The Cuban didn't answer. Frost lit up anyway.

Chapter Twenty

Ten minutes remained for the rendezvous, and though the one-eyed man had never landed at an impromptu airstrip with a cargo of drugs before, clandestine landings were not new to him. He realized there would be a formula to follow, a radio on the ground ready to receive and transmit landing codes and a fixed pattern of passes over the field. The wrong response, the wrong number of passes and the men on the ground would clear out and all Wilson and his men would have would be the cargo and a bunch of heavily armed and suspicious men who according to a court of law would have nothing to do with the illegal drugs and the explosives.

Frost turned to the Cuban pilot. "Now—I got a deal for you. I can tell my friends on the ground that you were cooperative, helped save my bacon back there—"

"Bacon?"

"My life—helped save my life back there in Colombia, the whole shot. Or, I can tell 'em about tryin' to push me out of the airplane, all sorts of horror stories. What'll it be?"

"I, ahh," the Cuban looked at him a moment. "You speak the truth—you will help me?"

Frost nodded, saying, "I speak the truth. I'll help you. All you've gotta do is make your recognition codes the right way and make the right approach and come in nice and easy. Once we're on the ground, I take the keys to the plane and you hide out of the way of the bullets. But you cross me, and I'll put a bullet right through your head. Okay?"

The pilot seemed to study Frost's face for a moment, then nodded. "Si—I will help you."

"Then get on the radio as soon as you're supposed to and start the ball rolling—and remember," and Frost gestured with the Metalifed High Power. "I speak Spanish. Not fluently, but well enough to sort out the razzle dazzle from the bullshit. Right?"

"Si," and the pilot took the radio microphone, then leaned down and flipped through the channels, stopping then and picking up the microphone.

In Spanish, only slightly too fast for Frost to comprehend every word, the Cuban pilot said, "Condor to Bulldog, Condor to Bulldog—request old friend. Condor to Bulldog, Condor to Bull-dog—request old friend. Over."

Static broke on the air, then a voice, American sounding, called out, "Condor, this is Bulldog—old friend waiting for you as designated. Give greeting."

Frost looked at the Cuban pilot. The "greeting" would be a code word that all was well, and then there would be a combination recognition and code word from the ground, giving the signal to land. The one-eyed man had no idea what the code word would be, nor could he tell if the pilot would give the correct one. The pilot waited, while the man on the ground repeated the call.

"Remember," Frost rasped, gesturing with his pistol. "Friend and you get off easy—enemy and you get off dead."

"Si," the pilot answered, then said the word, "Suelte," or "relax." "Los numeros—cuatro, siete, cataorce, veinte, tres, diez y seis. Repeat—"

Frost stopped the man, holding his hand so he couldn't depress the push-to-talk button.

"What the—"

"Numbers—a set of numbers, picked at random—a different set for each day of the year—and he will give me the name of a part of the body and a number, so I will know—"

"Condor—this is bulldog—did not receive your repetition," the American voice said in Spanish. Then, "Frente—ocho," or "forehead—eight."

"Si, Bulldog," the pilot answered, then started to work his controls for the descent. For the thousandth or so time in his life, Frost told himself he had to learn to fly. He made a mental promise to do so as soon as possible.

But he had seen enough of controls being operated, even handled them enough to know what the pilot was doing—he was starting to take the craft down in altitude, for a pass or two at the field and then the landing.

Frost glanced at his wristwatch. From the sound of the radio communication and the rapidity with which the pilot began the landing process, the one-eyed man assumed they were getting close—he showed three minutes left until the supposed touchdown time.

Frost looked at the Browning High Power in his hand. If Lew Wilson hadn't made it in time, that was all that separated life from death, that and a pilot he intended to cold cock the first second the wheels stopped rolling. If Wilson had made it, Frost was "grown-up" enough to know the drill. The men would have to be boarding the plane for the cargo before Wilson and his anti-drug strike force people would move. It would be that way, regardless of Wilson's desire for Frost to stay alive. Otherwise, if the shooting started earlier, the bust would be blown. The men on the ground needed contact with the goods aboard the plane. It had to be, to make a case that would stand up in court.

Frost assessed his chances as the pilot started down out of the clouds, and below him the one-eyed man could see the tops of palm trees, greenness everywhere and beyond it, a reddish swatch cut in the ground, a yellow colored bulldozer even now finishing clearing the landscape for the safe landing of the plane.

The bulldozer had two purposes, the one-eyed man realized. If the plane crashed, the bulldozer would bury it and the occupants and then be taken away. A missing man, a missing plane—perhaps the Bermuda Triangle? Who could say, except the man who drove the bulldozer.

Frost had his Browning High Power and plenty of spare magazines. There were spare magazines for an M-16 in his pack—but he had no M-16. There was his knife. A gun, a knife—a slim margin against death.

He could feel the drop in altitude, the plane passing over the field now and the pilot playing with the controls. Frost could feel, see, the plane dipping its portside wing and starting to bank. Would they land now, or make another pass instead?

It was the landing. He could see the pilot throttling back the controls, watching the RPMs.

Frost felt his palms sweat, thankful for the rubber

stickiness of the Pachmayr grips on his pistol — at least he could hold the gun.

On the field, as the plane descended and the pilot worked the controls with equivalent skill to a brain surgeon with a scalpel, Frost could see three automobiles — one of them a convertible.

"We are going in, señor," the pilot murmured.

Frost nodded, saying nothing, his right fist balling around the butt of the Browning.

If Wilson hadn't made it yet, Frost knew his goose would be cooked. As the plane came ever closer to touchdown, he could count the number of men visible — at least a dozen. One semi-automatic pistol against twelve men was poor odds in anyone's book.

The pilot was performing his magic act again with the controls, the plane's power cutting back — Frost imagined because of the shortness of the field. He could see the shadow of the craft under them now, growing larger, larger, and then the shadow all but vanished as Frost heard the skidding sound of the aircraft tires against the dirt runway. The landing was bumpy, the track beneath the plane uneven. Frost found himself holding the arm of the co-pilot's seat so tightly with his left hand that when he looked down, the skin under his nails had changed color and his knuckles were white.

"Relax, señor — I have landed in far worse places."

Frost looked at the man a moment, then smiled. He really did sort of like him, he reflected, already feeling bad for what he must do.

The plane was down, and taxiing, the four men standing beside one of the cars climbing aboard, three men beside the other car doing the same, both cars starting across into the field, toward the aircraft. The convertible was already moving, four men visible in it. And at the far end of the field, beside the bulldozer and a large truck apparently designed to haul it, Frost could see the twelfth man.

The plane started to slow, then lurched once and stopped, turned back into the wind.

"Do you shut down?"

"No — I leave the engine running — in case there is a need to take off again quickly."

"Makes sense," Frost nodded, then as the pilot turned away, looking out his open storm window toward the ground, Frost crashed the butt of the High Power down at the base of the man's skull, rasping, "Sorry pal — but the rest of the deal's still on."

The pilot slumped forward, over the controls, and Frost pulled his head back, putting him into a more upright sitting position.

Frost unbuckled his seat belt, his left hand holding the High Power now, his right hand on the co-pilot's side door.

They would expect him to get out of the plane — soon. And he looked nothing like the American smuggler who should have been riding there. Not even the clothes were similar.

Frost threw open the door, as though preparing to exit, shifting the High Power back to his right fist as the convertible pulled up alongside.

From the outside mirror on the co-pilot's side, he could see the men in the convertible — three wore shoulder holsters, including the driver. The fourth man carried a riot shotgun. "Ohh," the one-eyed man groaned.

"Lew," he murmured. "Hurry up."

Frost watched as the one with the riot shotgun who had sat beside the driver and the driver started toward his side of the plane, the other two coming around behind.

Frost heard the cargo door opening and looked behind him.

One of the four men from the convertible had his hands on the bales of marijuana as Frost's and his eyes met.

"You're not—"

Frost smiled and shot the man in the chest as he reached for his gun, then wheeled in his seat, firing point blank at his most dangerous adversary—the man with the riot shotgun.

Frost jumped from the plane, tackling the driver of the convertible as the man struggled a revolver from his shoulder rig.

Frost's right fist slammed outward, the butt of the High Power connecting with the tip of the driver's jaw, the man going down.

Gunfire was starting now from the edge of the field, and one of the two sedans was speeding past the nose of the airplane, the windows open, men firing— toward him.

Frost hit the dirt, grabbing the riot shotgun from the dead man beside the plane.

He tromboned the pump and rolled, a burst of sub-machinegun fire impacting beside him against the ground.

Frost shouldered the riot pump, firing. It was a slug load from the feel of it and from the gaping hole the round made in the windshield of the sedan. The sedan swerved, out of control.

Frost pumped the shotgun again, swinging it toward the tail of the aircraft, the last of the four men from the convertible coming around from the rear of the craft, firing a pistol.

Frost's right arm stung, but Frost fired the riot shotgun, from the hip. This time, it was buckshot—from what it did to the face and neck of the gunman, Frost figured the size as somewhere between number four and double 0 in size—roughly the difference between .25 and .30 caliber for each pellet.

Frost pumped the shotgun—guessing the next round up would be a slug again.

He shouldered the weapon toward the second car, but then dropped to the dirt, a helicopter zooming across the field, then another. There was the sound of gunfire from his far right and Frost looked toward the sound. Three cars were on the field, and hanging from the open door of a pickup truck in their lead was Lew Wilson, his pistol firing toward the third car.

The right front tire of the third car blew out, and the car started swerving.

Wilson disappeared inside the cab of the pickup, then the pickup swerved hard right, cutting off the sedan, the sedan rolling along on the rim, the two vehicles crashing, shuddering and stopping.

Frost picked himself up, dusting the dirt from the front of his cammie pants, then realizing it was useless.

One of the helicopters still hovered over the field, a bullhorn announcing, "We are Federal and State officers—you are under arrest. You are ordered to lay down your arms."

The second helicopter had already landed, men in

flak vests carrying M-16s surrounding the first sedan, the one with the shot-out windshield.

Frost looked at the riot shotgun in his hands, then started to unload the magazine tube. Emptied, he worked the slide release and extracted the live round in the chamber—it was a slug. He snapped the trigger on the empty chamber and rested the shotgun against the side of the airplane—it was one of his favorites, the Mossberg 500 ATP6P.

Frost walked toward the truck and the second sedan, the front fenders seeming as though the vehicles were copulating.

Wilson was climbing down from the cab, but coming out through the driver's side.

He looked at Frost, pushing his glasses back from the bridge of his nose.

"See the way I shot out that tire, with this," and he smiled, raising his Beretta 92SB.

Frost lit a Camel in the blue yellow flame of his Zippo, then through a mouthful of smoke as he spoke, rasped, "Lucky shot—Lew, a lucky shot."

Chapter Twenty-one

"We're gonna make it as easy as we can on that Cuban pilot—maybe just deport him since he's a Cuban citizen."

"Thanks, Lew," Frost smiled. The one-eyed man sipped at his drink—a Seven and Seven—and then lit a cigarette.

"That was one hell of a story—and that Miranda Ceballos—sounds like somethin' else."

"Hey," Frost noted. "I wasn't even supposed to tell you anything about this—so keep what you don't need to use—keep it under your hat. Or Joe'll be pissed."

"Joe—yeah, good old Joe. He's a character, isn't he."

"Yeah—a hell of a lot of fun, dynamite conversationalist—the whole ball of wax."

"What's the matter?" Wilson asked.

"I don't know—I should feel good about this thing, but I don't. You know."

"Look—maybe one of those guys was nailed out there at the field—maybe he'll talk and we'll get a line on where the rest of the explosives went. Looks like there were three more shipments unaccounted for that did get in—at least. Enough explosives to blow up a couple of city blocks. But you did good."

"Ahh—if I knew what I went there to learn, then I would have done good."

"So you still don't know—if Oriana Vasquez had her father knocked off."

"No—I still don't know," Frost responded.

"What are you gonna do, then?"

"Much as I hate to say it," Frost smiled, studying his drink, "I guess if she's guilty, she'll get away with it. When I hadda croak Barranca—well, there just wasn't the time to sweat anything out of him. So, if he did pull the strings on Oriana, I guess—" and Frost let the idea hang. Then he asked Wilson, "What's she been up to anyway?"

"Open war practically—between her people and the pro-Castro elements—and her people seem to be gettin' the worst of it. She's no strategist."

"And she's not worth one-tenth as much as her father. He was a fine old man," Frost nodded, sipping at his drink.

"Yeah—Moises Vasquez was respected by everybody —I even think by the people he fought. He was a smart man, tough—but—"

"But I guess we all get it eventually, don't we," Frost nodded, finishing his drink.

"Hey—since I'm buyin', you plannin' to eat too?"

Frost laughed, then looked at the menu. "Yeah— I'll eat." It was the same restaurant where they'd eaten before, and Frost was tempted to order steak and crab legs again, but decided on something else—filet of Dover Sole Almandine. It was one seafood dish he really enjoyed if it were prepared right. Once, in Denver, he'd eaten it and just before the waiter had finished preparing it at the tableside brazier the waiter had poured barbecue sauce on it. Frost had been someone's guest—a man he'd worked for—and eaten it, but the ruining of the fish with the sauce had been unforgivable. "They don't throw barbecue sauce on stuff here, do they?"

"Only if it's something like ribs—why?"

"Just checkin' out the possibilities for Dover Sole Almandine."

"It's terrific here," Wilson interrupted. "I'll have that too."

They ordered the food and while they waited, Frost studied the wharf outside the window of the restaurant, the seagulls again buzzing the people who walked there. Finally, as Frost lit another cigarette, Wilson said, "Hank—I'd like you to do me a favor—before you go."

"Sure—if I can," Frost nodded, inhaling the smoke into his lungs. "What is it—pick up the tab for the next dinner?"

"No," Wilson laughed. "No—all it'll cost is a little gasoline or cab fare and a little time."

"What?" Frost asked again.

"I want you to go see Oriana Vasquez—"

"What—and wring her neck—my—"

"No," Wilson interrupted, then stopped as the food came.

Frost tasted the Sole—it was delicious. "Good," he murmured, then waited as Wilson began again.

"I want you to ask her something for me—I can't get in to see her. Figured maybe you could. Tell her about killing Barranca or something—to get her to see you. But I really need your help."

"Get her to cool things?" Frost asked.

"Yeah—she's gotta or it's gonna come down hard all over South Florida. I mean, we don't have any evidence to arrest her, but we know it's her people who are knocking off some of the pro-Castro elements, and we know a lot of her people are gettin' zapped. And if I did arrest her, or Miami PD did it—well, things wouldn't go too well. If you know what I mean."

"Fun city, huh—yeah—I know," Frost nodded.

"Can you do it?"

"You hire a mercenary—for free already—as a peace envoy—you're silly."

"Will you do it?"

Frost looked at his fish and put down his fork, taking a swallow of his fresh drink.

"Yeah—but if anyone else had asked me, I'd tell 'em where to—"

"I know—and I appreciate it."

Frost returned to his fish, trying to determine what he would say to her. "I know you killed your father, you lousy—" He decided that would be a bad opener. He looked across at Wilson, then said, "Lew—I don't think it's gonna do any good. I don't think she'll see me, and if she does, I don't think she'll listen. She's got the axe to grind in this thing, she's the one looking for the violence, and reason isn't gonna mean a damn to her. If I'm right, and she killed her father—then hell, this bloodbath is what she wanted all along."

Wilson nodded. "But I gotta try—you know that—it goes with the job."

Frost returned to eating his Sole—he knew it went with the job and he gave Wilson credit for it. If he could have had his way, the one-eyed man thought, he'd kill her and be done with it.

Chapter Twenty-two

Frost borrowed Wilson's car for the drive to Oriana Vasquez's stronghold—and it was that as he parked the car across the street from the gates and got out. He banged his bandaged right hand against the door handle and snapped his hand away, cursing, his right arm aching from the bullet graze there. "Shit," he snapped, angry with himself for going to see her.

He flexed his right hand, the pain ebbing as he did. The underside of his second finger and the Venus mound beneath the thumb had been cut by the slide of the automatic pistol when he'd grabbed for it there on the plane, and though the cuts weren't deep and simple dressings protected them, there was still some pain.

The bandages didn't interfere with the use of his pistol. Frost left his jacket open as he walked across the street, Oriana's guards seeing him. He thought he might need it.

He recognized the man coming toward him—Alberto?

"Alberto," Frost murmured.

"Señor Frost—you should not be here."

"One question, Juan—when you dumped me. Were you supposed to kill me?"

"No—now leave."

"Sure thing," Frost smiled, feigning to haul his right back for a haymaker, but snapping out his left foot, catching the big bodyguard in the crotch with the instep of his foot.

Alberto doubled over and Frost reached under the man's coat, breaking out both of the matching Smith Model 66 2½s, shoving him away and levelling both revolvers at the guards now running toward him.

None of the men made for their weapons, waiting, and Frost rasped, "Now—tell the lady of the house—tell her she's got a gentleman caller and if she doesn't let me in, she's minus a few bodyguards. Right?"

Alberto was starting to stir at his feet, and Frost kicked him once in the side of the head. "He moves again before one of you gets back with Oriana and it's a bullet out of one of his own guns next time—now get her!"

Frost lowered one of the muzzles—the gun in his left hand—toward the unconscious man at his feet, the other trained on the bodyguards. "At this distance, no matter how many of you start shooting at me, I can't miss him. And it's good-bye Al, hello cemetery."

One of the guards started edging away, murmuring, "Si—I will get Señorita Vasquez—she can kill you."

"Yeah—you do that," Frost smiled. "Just do that."

He had no intention of killing Al—they were even for the crack on the back of the head he had given Frost with the rifle butt. But the longer the situation dragged on, the more certain the guards would be that he had no intention of pulling a trigger. With nine of them now and one of him, he didn't like the odds for a fistfight. He waited—for Oriana.

Frost couldn't shift the position of his guns to tell the time, but he judged a full five minutes—tense minutes—had passed, and then the man who had gone for Oriana reappeared and behind him, coming through the tunnel-like outside entrance hall, was Oriana. She wore an ankle length dress—a lounging outfit perhaps—Frost couldn't tell, and her dark hair was down to her shoulders.

"Since you seem so determined to come someplace where you are unwelcome, I suppose I have no choice—you may come in. But leave the guns."

"No," Frost told her. "See, after we're through talking I want to be able to leave in one piece. Being tossed down in the Keys in the middle of nowhere and getting rolled by some dopeheads may be your idea of fun, but once was enough for me," Frost smiled.

Oriana visibly shrugged. "Very well—show your immaturity even further—come in fully armed, and be certain to have a gun trained on me at all times. I may be deadly." She turned and started walking back into the house.

Frost called after her, "Oriana—you are—deadly."

He walked past the ten standing guards, stepping across the body of the unconscious Alberto, the guns trained on the men, then walked into the tunnel-like hall and followed Oriana through the open doorway into the house. He kicked the door closed, shoved one of the revolvers in his belt and closed the lock on the door.

Oriana was looking at him, strangely. "Anyone in the house?"

"My maid—she might attempt to garrote you with the strings of her apron."

"Good point," Frost smiled. "I'll watch out for that. Let's go talk."

"The library?"

"Yes," Frost nodded, staring after her, shoving the second revolver into his belt opposite the first one.

She waited beside the open library doors and Frost stopped. "Go ahead—ladies first, Oriana," he told her.

She disappeared inside, Frost glancing around the hallway, then he followed her.

Frost closed the library doors after him, then surveyed the room. By the fireplace were the two chess tables—the one, with conventional chess, where he had played with Moises Vasquez, and the second, with three-dimensional chess—Vasquez had promised to teach him.

"Do you play chess, Oriana?"

"Of course," she nodded, going to a small bar in the corner and pouring a drink from a decanter that looked like crystal. "Should I offer you a drink?"

"Only if I pour and the bottle's a fresh one that I pick."

She smiled, gesturing toward the bottles behind her. "Anything you wish—from the bar."

Frost walked across the room, selecting an unopened bottle of V.O. and twisting it open, then pouring a glass. "Have you come for your severance pay?" she asked. "I understand mercenaries are very interested in their money—more than anything else."

"I didn't come for money. I came to talk."

"You have no one else to talk with, besides a woman who despises you?"

"You trying to say you blame me for the death of your father?"

"That should be obvious—it was your incompetence—"

"And your shawl—when you dropped it," Frost smiled. He watched her bare shoulders tense, the tiny muscles around her eyes doing the same.

"You are—"

"I am right," Frost told her. "But relax—I can't prove it."

"You are insane—leave my—"

"Your father's house, you mean? No—not yet. And if you push some panic button and get your men in here, I'll shoot you first. Just the excuse I want. But I didn't come for that—I came just to talk."

She tossed her hair with a shake of her head and walked back toward the bar, pouring herself another drink. "About what?"

"About what you're doing."

"Ohh—Señor Wilson asked you to come."

"Yeah—Lew asked me to. Otherwise, if I'd never seen you again it would have been too soon."

"And what is it that Señor Wilson proposes—that I tell my men not to defend—"

"You're sending your men out, puttin' the arm on the pro-Castro people, trying to start a war. It's intentional, and the men who worked for your father are so loyal to his memory they're doing it, because you tell them to. You're sending your father's men to their death. Brave men, good men, men fighting against Castro and all the crap he stands for. And you're gettin' 'em knocked off. And innocent people are gonna start gettin' killed. You—you're doing it. And Lew asked me to ask you to stop. I told him it wouldn't do any good—that you wanted a damned war—that was why you killed your father in—"

She cut him off, almost breaking her glass as she set it down hard on top of the bar. "Stop that—I didn't kill him!"

"No—you didn't pull the trigger, you had somebody else do it. Blow your own father's head apart like an over-ripe—"

"Shut up," she screamed.

"Are you gonna stop this—this little war of yours?"

"It was started long before my father died—and it will continue."

There was banging at the library doors, Frost grabbing the revolvers from his belt. Oriana called out, "I am all right—return to your post."

There was a muffled "Si Señorita Vasquez?" and Frost turned from the doors, putting away the revolvers once again.

"I will walk you safely outside," she told him.

"I can't change your mind?"

"What was started so many years ago cannot be undone for a word, a wish—I will change nothing. I can change nothing."

The one-eyed man looked at her a moment, then whispered, "So beautiful and so evil—I hope you rot in hell," and he started walking after her through the library doors.

She stopped, looked at him and for one of the few times since he'd met her, she smiled. "That is where I live, I have lived and I will always live—hell, a hell you cannot know," and she walked away.

Chapter Twenty-three

Frost had returned Wilson's car, but refused the offer of a lift, taking a cab back across to Miami Beach and then walking, rather than taking the cab all the way back to his shoreside hotel.

In a week or so, Bess would be back Stateside and he would meet her. He'd probably look up Mike O'Hara, his friend from the FBI, sometime later. There were things to do, things to make him forget what was happening in Miami and would keep on happening under Oriana Vasquez.

He stopped walking, looking up and finding himself at his hotel. He walked inside, asking at the lobby desk if there had been any messages—there were none. Then, still not wanting to go to his room, he walked across the lobby and out, through the gardens there and beyond, to the beach.

It was late, and no one swam, the temperature too cool for native Floridians to venture into the ocean and the tourist trade apparently elsewhere. He walked along a cement walkway, paralleling the sand, a bench nearby. He dusted the sand from it—he had ruined enough clothes this time out—and sat down, thinking.

It was something about what Oriana Vasquez had said—about living a hell he could never understand. He wondered what she had meant. There were all sorts of private hells—the one-eyed man knew that well. But what kind of a personal hell would make a woman set up her own father for assassination, make her betray something her father had worked so hard for.

The few times in his life Frost had seen his father, they had never gotten along, but the thought of killing his own father had never once crossed Frost's mind. There were things people didn't do—even the worst of people. It was like the children under the Nazi regime in Germany who betrayed their parents to the party—unthinkable.

Frost lit a cigarette, inhaling deeply, then watching the smoke as he exhaled, as the breeze blowing across the bench caught it and made it dissipate.

What drove Oriana Vasquez? Frost asked himself again.

She was beautiful, rich, intelligent—she had gone to the best—

"Schools," Frost murmured. "Oh my God—no."

The one-eyed man stood up, running back toward the lobby, going to the desk, conniving the man behind the desk to let him use the house phone. "It's a police emergency," he told the clerk.

The phone rang, rang, rang—then the voice, sleepy-sounding, irritable.

"Lew—Hank. Meet me for a drink and get on the horn to any really good reporter you know—have him call me at my hotel right away—I need to know something. Maybe somebody with connections in the Cuban community, or a society columnist."

"Hank—"

"Just do it—I'll be in the lobby," and Frost hung up.

He could feel his palms sweating.

He walked back and forth across the lobby, watching the black face of the Rolex, comparing it to the digital Rolex clock in the lobby.

Ten minutes—"Mr. Frost—I have a call for you at the—"

Frost was beside the front desk, taking the phone across the desk from the clerk.

"Am I talking to a Mr. Frost?" the woman's voice on the other end of the line asked.

"Yes—are you a—"

"I'm a reporter—Lew Wilson asked me—do you know what time it is?"

Frost looked at his watch. "One A.M.—almost. Look—I'm sorry—but it's important—to Lew and to me—gotta know something, tonight."

"What?" the sleepy sounding voice came back.

"I think I remember someone telling me—her father. But I have to know for sure—tonight. What university did Oriana Vasquez attend—and when?"

"What? You must be—"

"I have to know—I'll be in the bar here—with Lew—can you call me—how long?"

"Wait," the woman's voice said. "Yes—maybe an hour."

"All right—thanks," and Frost hung up the telephone. If he was right, he knew it all.

Chapter Twenty-four

The call came ten minutes before Lew Wilson—looking as though he hadn't slept—which he hadn't—arrived.

Frost still sat at the bar. Wilson sat down beside him. "What the hell is—"

"I know," Frost told Wilson.

"Know what—I mean, hey—if I'm slow I'm sorry. I been up eighteen hours. There was a—what the hell—you don't care. You know what—what?"

"I don't have any proof—but I know."

"What do you know—or been drinkin'?"

"This is the only drink I've had," Frost answered, gesturing to his half-empty glass. "Except for the drink I had a couple hours ago with Oriana."

"Hell of a lot of good that did—two more of her men turned up shot to death—she doesn't know—"

"She knows—exactly what she's doing. I need you to contact Joe."

"Joe?"

"Yeah—and you gotta ask him a question and get a straight answer—and we'll have it all knocked if he comes up with the right answer."

"What are you talkin' about?"

"I been set up—all along. Not by you—you were the only one who didn't. The only one."

"Set up for what?" Wilson asked.

"Lew—Oriana attended Fallworth College for Women."

"So what? A lot of dames do—probably why it's a college for women," Wilson laughed.

"Lew—so did Miranda Ceballos—Miranda and Oriana, same college, same years. Both women from a Spanish-speaking background—small college. Would have known each other—"

"So—a coincidence."

"Tell me something," Frost asked. "Was Oriana ever engaged? Or married?"

"No—I don't think so. Why? What the hell has any of this got—"

"I need you to ask Joe two questions—and maybe they both have the same answer. And I don't care if you gotta pound the crap out of him—get straight answers. Agreed?"

"Yeah—agreed—what?"

"First—why did he really send me down to knock off Emilio Barranca—"

"That's—"

"And second," Frost insisted—taking a sip of his drink—looking at Lew, "I need to know what he thought of Miranda Ceballos before I went down there, what he thinks of her now and anything he can tell me about her father's death."

"What—you're not making much sense, Hank—"

"Lew—do it and they'll give you a bigger office."

"My office is fine."

Then Frost remembered what he'd told Joe back on the beach when they'd talked. "Tell Joe I sent you to collect my leather medal."

The one-eyed man downed his drink and looked at his watch. After a quick, cold shower, the timing would be perfect.

Chapter Twenty-five

Frost had decided to do it perfectly.

He wore tight-fitting black jeans, tucked into the tops of his black combat boots. A black knit shirt, long-sleeved, buttoned to the throat, the Rolex under the cuff of the knit shirt so the luminous face wouldn't betray his presence.

He'd taken a removable field blue and painted the Metalifed High Power, wearing the Cobra Comvest harness and taking a piece of black electrical tape and securing the holster against the side of his shirt to guard against noise.

He had field-blued the blade of the Gerber knife as well, and the exposed metal of the thumbreak on its sheath, as well as the nickel-plated steel belt chip.

On his hands, he wore black cloth gloves, fingerless, his hands camouflaged black where the skin would show. His face was camouflage painted as well—in black. And it itched, his allergy to camouflage paint and the itching it caused something he had resigned himself to never escaping.

Across his face, covering his nose and below to his mouth, was a black bandanna, knotted behind his neck, and covering his hair was an identical bandanna, tied pirate fashion—or Ninja fashion, depending on the period one preferred, Frost thought. He had never moved silently enough to call himself anything like a Ninja, but he was silent for normal men.

He had climbed up into the tree when two of the guards had stopped to share a light, and now, from his perch he could see the top of the stone wall, six-feet away.

Oriana might be in, or might be out—but her little sportscar was gone, and so was one of the cars the guards rode in. So he assumed she was out. If she were in, it could prove awkward.

There would be the maid—perhaps her night off, or perhaps she didn't sleep in? Frost didn't know. He would deal with her if necessary.

He waited as two of the guards disappeared into the shadow beside the front gate, and then he jumped, landing on the flat top surface of the wall, his feet on the jagged glass fragments there, balancing himself so he wouldn't put his hands on them.

He jumped then, down from the wall, the ten feet to the ground below.

He looked in the darkness at the soles of his boots—they hadn't cut on the glass.

He raised up from a crouch and flattened himself against the wall. There was always the possibility Oriana had belatedly taken the advice her father had ignored when Frost had given it—install an electronic security system. But Moises Vasquez had refused and Frost hoped Oriana Vasquez hadn't bothered.

Frost held his breath, listening—there was no sound, other than the sounds of the night—crickets rubbing their knees together, the rustling of leaves in the slight breeze.

Frost pushed away from the wall and started

moving across the grounds. Inevitably, there would be guards on the grounds—he would have to put them out, he knew.

Frost stopped beside a palm tree, his eyes accustomed to the darkness well enough to make out the details of the grounds. Ahead of him was the back of the house, the house wall perhaps twenty-five yards from him, running up toward the front entrance tunnel, then there was the driveway beyond. It wouldn't be open as it had been earlier.

That he viewed as an advantage—whatever happened to slow the guards on the outside from getting inside was to his benefit.

Frost started moving ahead, toward the house wall. He got ten yards and froze, then dropped flat to the ground. He heard the crunch of footsteps. He mentally debated whether to pull his knife, but he had no quarrel with Oriana's men, men doing their duty just as he would. He waited, in the shadow on the ground, listening.

The footsteps were louder, at an angle to him, whoever it was walking closer to the house wall.

Frost gauged the sound, waiting until it reached its peak and started to decline. He pushed himself up on his hands, his right arm still hurting but no pain in his right hand.

He hurtled himself toward the figure of the guard, his left hand snaking out and brushing aside the shotgun muzzle, his right hand hammering into the base of the jaw. The man's head snapped back, against the wall, the shotgun falling, Frost catching it, then sliding the body to the ground. He felt the back of the head. It wasn't wet with blood, and there was a strong pulse. He eased the man all the way down, pulling the body into some bushes and leaving it there after removing the handgun worn on the hip. He emptied the gun and tossed it into the bushes—a Smith K-frame revolver. He emptied the shotgun—another Mossberg—and dropped the shells for that and the revolver in the bushes, then left the shotgun.

Frost started moving again, along the house wall.

He was nearing the back door, the servants' entrance or whatever Oriana now called it. There was sound in the kitchen and light and he peered through a window. He saw the maid, but not complete with black uniform and white cap, standing at the sink. She wore instead a robe, ankle length. She was getting something—he couldn't tell what.

Frost rolled back the cuff of his shirt. It was four-thirty—he supposed she could have been an early riser. He didn't know.

He heard footsteps again. Frost flattened himself against the house wall, waiting.

Just past the back door the wall stopped and angled off, and the footsteps came from beyond the corner made by the wall. Frost edged closer to the corner.

The man passed him, and Frost's hands snaked out, his left arm going around the throat, his right knee hammering into the small of the back, his right hand going over the mouth. Frost brought him down, released his grip of the mouth and laced his right fist across the jaw, the head lolling to the side.

Frost felt under the man's lightweight windbreaker, finding a pistol in a shoulder holster. Frost pulled the gun and emptied it—a Walther PPK/S—and worked the slide, emptying it as well.

He lowered the trigger guard, edging it against the frame and pulled the slide back, then up and ran it forward, the slide dismounted from the frame. He tossed the frame one way and the slide the other, into the darkness, the gun useless.

He pulled the body closer to the house wall, behind more of the bushes, and left it.

He approached the back door. The maid apparently had a sweet tooth, he smiled—she was drinking a glass of milk and eating what looked like chocolate cake. Eating cake at four-thirty in the morning was enough to nauseate him. He shrugged, then walked closer to the door. There would be the day-shift guards, sleeping in the house, but aside from the maid, there would be no one awake—he hoped.

Frost took his pistol from the leather, then rapped one of the glass panes in the back door hard with the butt, the glass shattering, Frost punching his hand through the door and freeing the lock.

The maid dropped her glass of milk, standing up, but Frost was through the door, the pistol pointed at her.

"Shh," he murmured. "Relax—Conchita," he told her.

"Señor—"

"Si—I won't hurt you. Now—take off your robe."

"But—"

"Do it," and he gestured with the pistol. There was always the chance the single pane of glass breaking had alerted someone, or the sound of the glass of milk falling, though the glass hadn't broken. But he assumed he'd gotten both waking guards patrolling the interior grounds, and the other men would be sleeping—he hoped very soundly.

Conchita began removing her robe, a full length nightgown underneath.

"Now sit down—in the chair where you were," Frost told her.

She obeyed. He took the robe and ripped, pulling off one of the sleeves. This, to tie across her mouth, then used the belt from the robe to tie her hands behind her in the chair. "You'll be fine—when the men come down for breakfast or the Señorita returns, you'll be found—relax."

He ripped the other sleeve, bent down and began to tie her ankles together. She giggled. Frost looked up at her quizzically. "You look silly—and my ankles are ticklish."

Frost smiled, realizing she couldn't see it under the bandanna across his face.

He finished tying her ankles and stood up. "How old are you, Conchita?"

"Seventeen," she smiled.

"Stay healthy kid," and he tied the ripped sleeve of the robe across her mouth. "Can you breathe?"

She nodded in the affirmative and Frost patted her on the shoulder, "See ya sometime."

He started from the kitchen, the pistol in his right hand, ready. Beyond the kitchen door the house was dark, except for a single light in the hallway. He imagined the maid had left it on. Beyond the circle of light he could see the base of the stairs. Frost started toward them.

At the base of the stairs he waited, listening. There were no sounds other than the ticking of the clock in the hallway and the humming of the air conditioning. He started up the stairs, two at a time, hugging the wall side to reduce the possibility of a stair tread creaking under his weight.

He reached the top, flattening himself against the hall wall in the darkness, waiting.

His target was the little office Oriana's father had liked to use on the second floor—he imagined Oriana used it herself these days.

Frost started away from the wall, toward it, then stopped. There was someone coming from the far end of the hallway, where the bodyguard's rooms were. And he could hear the sound of a toilet flushing.

He waited in the shadow of a doorway, listening. The footsteps came closer. He could see the man now, rubbing his stomach—hungry? "Great," Frost almost said aloud. The man would go downstairs, see Conchita, then—As the man started down the steps, Frost reached out, grabbing a handful of hair with his left hand, his right fist snapping out against the jaw, the man's head whipping back.

Frost caught the body before it fell, easing it to the floor. On impulse, he rolled the body nearer to the top of the stairs, blocking the top stair with it.

Frost glanced at his watch. Almost five A.M. He started toward the small office, wondering where Oriana Vasquez was, but halfway knowing.

The office door was locked.

Frost cursed under his breath.

He leaned against the door, feeling it sag under his weight. He looked at the door again, then heaved his shoulder against it. The door gave and the cracking and splitting sound of the wood was only mildly loud. He started into the room, closing the door behind him. He wished life were like the movies—the good guy always had a lock pick set and knew how to use it.

Frost reached under his shirt, extracting the Safariland Kel-Lite flashlight stuffed into his belt. Shielding the beam with his hand, he turned it on, aiming it around the room. It was different than when Moises Vasquez had used it—wilted flowers on the desk, the curtains different—Oriana was using it now. He felt a smile cross his lips.

Frost began searching the desk—it was not locked. In one drawer he found a stack of receipts. He started looking through them. He hadn't quite known what he was looking for when he'd come, but when he saw the blue receipt he knew he had found it—a rental receipt. He recognized the property address on the receipt as being a canal-side house up along the coast. They were the favorite haunts and warehouses of smugglers.

"Gotchya, lady," Frost murmured.

"Arriba sus manos!"

Frost wheeled, a man behind him with a gun. Frost's right hand crashed downward with the Kel-Lite, the aircraft aluminum tube of the light cracking across the man's gunhand wrist, the man screaming as the gun fell from his hand. Frost's right knee snapped up, catching the man in the crotch, doubling him over.

Frost ran for the door. As he stepped into the hallway, he could hear shouting, saw a man running toward him. Frost half wheeled, kicking out with his left foot, a double kick to the face of the guard, the body slumping back.

Frost started for the stairs, jumping the first tread and landing half on his feet in the stairwell, rolling down two steps, then flipping the railing and dropping to the hall floor.

There were more shouts behind him, then a scream, a body tumbling down the stairs as Frost looked back—someone had tripped on the man he'd knocked out and left by the head of the stairs. A smile crossed his lips as he ran toward the front door.

Frost wrenched open the front door, two guards coming down the tunnel-like hallway.

Frost slammed the door and wheeled, throwing the bolt closed.

One of the guards from the second floor was down the stairs, a pistol coming up in his hands. Frost feigned a kick, then dove to the floor, doing a leg sweep with his right leg, the guard stumbling back. Frost was up, to his feet, his right foot lashing out, kicking away the gun, then snapping back, then kicking again for the side of the head.

Frost jumped the body, dodging a burst of pistol fire hammering into the far wall of the downstairs hall as he ran toward the kitchen.

Frost burst through the kitchen door—Conchita was still there.

He ripped the gag loose of her mouth and pinched her behind.

"Scream, honey!"

She screamed, Frost waiting by the inside of the kitchen door.

The door burst open, a man running through, closely followed by another.

Frost kicked the second man in the rear end, sending him sprawling, then stepped into the wide-open guard of the first man as he turned around.

Frost's left hand hammered down in a knife-edge blow across the gunhand wrist, knocking the gun aside, perhaps breaking the wrist, the heel of Frost's right hand smashing upward, against the base of the man's jaw. The man fell back.

Frost wheeled. The man he'd kicked was starting to his feet, a gun in his right hand. Frost made a wide kick, catching the man in the base of the jaw, the head slapping back against one of the lower level wooden kitchen cabinets.

"See ya, Conchita," Frost shouted, racing toward the back door, pulling it open and dashing into the back yard.

He could hear shouts, running footsteps.

Frost started for the wall, running for it in the darkness, suddenly feeling something reaching out for him, grabbing at him, hands and arms around his chest. It had to be Alberto—he was the only one big enough.

"I will kill—"

"Bullshit," Frost rasped, swelling his chest, then exhaling, dipping down out of the bear hug around him, hammering his left elbow into Alberto's crotch.

Frost could hear, feel the rush of air above him as Alberto doubled over. Frost wheeled, the toe of his left combat boot hammering against Alberto's right shin, then Frost's left fist straightarming into his chest, Frost's right chopping down along the left side of the neck, beside the ear. The big man started to topple and Frost hauled back with his left, then crossed his jaw with the fist. "Good-bye," Frost rasped, turning and starting to run again before the body could fall.

Frost made the wall, running toward the spot he had told Moises Vasquez to have fixed, the spot he hoped Oriana hadn't had fixed.

An unused doghouse, three feet from the side of the wall and three and one-half feet high. Frost reached it and jumped, hoping the roof would hold, feeling it crumble under him as he reached out for the tree branch that grew over the wall.

His right hand had it, but his left slipped. Frost threw his arm up, getting a grip with his left finally, then swinging his legs up and out. His feet reached the top of the wall and Frost pushed himself up, cutting his hands on the broken glass there.

There was no choice but to jump now, and Frost dropped down into the darkness on the far side of the wall.

Something was under him as he hit, something big, bumpy-feeling in the darkness, and suddenly hands were reaching out for him, grabbing at his throat. Frost smashed his right elbow back, hearing a groaning sound behind him in the darkness as he rolled right. Frost hit the dirt, semi-automatic assault rifle fire came from behind him, loud now.

Frost rolled onto his back, pushing himself to his feet as the shadowy figure less than a yard from him lunged. Frost's left fist flailed out, feigning a punch, the figure dodging away from it as Frost snapped his right out, the heel of his hand finding something that squished under it in the darkness. There was a sound like a scream as Frost sidestepped, wheeled and snapped his left foot up and back, his ankle and knee taking the shockwave as his foot punched against something hard. Frost turned and ran, pistol shots ringing behind him. He looked back once and in the darkness saw the flash from a burst of gun fire, the tongues of flame blindingly bright in the darkness.

Frost tripped once, over an exposed tree root, cursing under his breath as he pushed himself to his feet, running again.

Then he could see it, the car straight ahead of him, the car he had rented just for the possibility that he would need to escape in a hurry. It was black, just like the clothing the one-eyed man wore. As Frost fumbled the door key and slid behind the wheel, he could see shadows coming toward him through the darkness. He fingered the electric door button and turned the key, the Pontiac Firebird's big Crossfire Fuel-Injected 305 V8 thundering now.

He worked the console-mounted mirror switch on his right—the mirror showing headlights behind him on the street where he had parked. He could guess who was driving—some of Oriana's men.

Frost cranked the automatic transmission into drive as he released the emergency brake, stomping the gas pedal hard, the velvety black Trans Am seeming to pulse around him as he flicked the headlight switch and laid rubber. The men rushing the car jumped back, gunfire echoing dully from outside, the sound of bullets pinging off the side of the body work as he streaked the car past them.

A car was ahead of him, swerving hard to block the street. Frost wrenched the wheel hard right, taking the car up and over the curb, the posi-traction rear end biting into the grass and sand past the curb as Frost hammered down the accelerator.

The car lurched ahead, Frost cutting the wheel

hard left and back onto the street. The car that had blocked the street was coming around, stopping suddenly by the shuddering of the headlights, more headlights passing it.

He had mapped out his potential escape route carefully, and as he reached the nearest corner, the one-eyed man cut the wheel sharp, hitting the emergency brake, the car skidding hard left. Frost released the emergency brake, accelerating up the street along a broad palm-studded residential area. The sun was just starting to rise, the horizon grey in front of him. Behind him, in the still-total darkness, he could see the headlights of the cars following him, one set of headlights seeming to make a barrel roll, then one of the lights going out suddenly. The one-eyed man smiled—one of his pursuers hadn't made the turn.

Frost counted the intersections as he passed them, picking up a set of Mars lights behind him—police. The one-eyed man smiled again—unless the police were ready for fighting combat troops, they'd have more than they bargained for with his pursuers.

Frost reached the intersection he wanted, the light red but little traffic on the street. He worked the emergency brake, cutting the wheel into a sharp right, the Trans Am's rear end fishtailing as he released the brake, then stomped on the gas. Even with the windows closed and the air conditioning on, he could hear the screech of his tires, the streaks of rubber visible in the arclights flooding the street as he looked in the rearview mirror.

The alley would be coming up soon, and Frost worked the emergency brake again, making a sharp left from as far to the right in the street as he could, seeing the headlights behind him and the Mars lights of the police car behind them. He released the brake, straightening out, fighting the wheel to thread the needle of the alley with the Pontiac.

Suddenly the alley walls were on both sides of him.

Frost smiled, accelerating, seeing the first set of headlights zig-zagging maddeningly as they started into the alley behind him.

Then suddenly they stopped. Frost worked the foot brake, the Pontiac slowing to a dead stop at the far end of the alley. He had to see it.

The alley space was too narrow for him to open the Pontiac's door, so he worked the power window, pulling the bandanna mask down from his face and the matching black scarf from his head. He could feel the corners of his mouth upturning in a smile under his mustache, as he heard the crunching of metal and shattering of glass. Three cars now were jammed into the alley opening, all of them full-sized cars, the kind favored for protection work, all of them jammed between the alley walls, unable to move.

He could see the Mars light behind them, the police car stuck as well.

Frost eased his head back into the car, congratulating himself. He had measured the widths of five alleys before selecting this particular one.

He killed the airconditioning, buttoning down the power windows and lighting a Camel in the blue yellow flame of his Zippo, then threw the transmission into drive.

As he put away the cigarettes, he felt the slip of

paper in his pocket — the rent receipt on the canal-side house.

Even though it was dawn, the night wasn't over yet.

Chapter Twenty-six

The one-eyed man poked his head above the water, gulping air through the filter of wet cloth covering the lower portion of his face. He tucked down again, under the water, breast stroking toward the edge of the canal. He pushed himself up above the surface of the water, looking again.

It was six-thirty A.M., the morning bright in the east, grey still in the west, no lights burning in the small house beyond the normal-seeming chain link fence. He pushed himself up, out of the water, streaking toward a hedgerow and hitting the dirt.

The Cobra shoulder rig was locked in the rented Trans Am, the High Power in a plastic bag taped to his chest. Frost ripped open the bag now, stuffing it into his pocket, working the slide on the High Power—slowly to cut down on noise—and leaving the hammer up. He upped the safety, peering up beyond the hedgerow toward the house.

If it were where the explosives were located, they would be armed—Frost tucked down, hearing a cracking sound.

He was cold in his wet clothes, and his feet were squishy-feeling inside the worn track shoes with which he'd replaced the black combat boots. He sucked in his breath hard, listening. Then he peered around the side of the hedgerow, toward the front of the house.

"Shit," he murmured to himself.

A man was standing on the porch, lighting a cigarette, and in the grey light a pistol was visible, stuffed in the front of the man's trousers.

"Why'd I have to get a damned early riser?" he asked himself, then looked away.

Frost stuck his own pistol into his trouser band, pulling the sodden and by now misshapen black knit shirt down over it. He would have to wait out the man, or take him quietly, as there were likely other men in the house.

Frost rolled back the cuff of his shirt, checking the luminous black face of the Rolex. Time was against him. Soon it would be fully light, and the odds on some of the other men in the house being awake would be higher.

And Oriana's whereabouts bothered him—could she be coming to the house? Could she have already removed the explosives if in fact they were stored there?

He made the decision—take the man now, while he was smoking, on the porch, relaxing, perhaps still fuzzy from the night's sleep or the lack of it.

Frost peered around the hedgerow again.

These men would be different from the bodyguards around Oriana's house. These men would know why the explosives were there, what they were intended for—they were Communists or working with them.

Frost mentally shrugged—killing Communists was like shooting holes in a trash can. There was little emotion involved.

He reached to the small of his back, for the little knife he carried there. Like the Metalifed High Power, it was wrapped in plastic. He pulled away the plastic, then took the knife from the sheath.

He watched the man on the porch intently—the cigarette looked burned down, nearly ready to be discarded.

Frost nodded slowly to himself.

It was time.

He clamped the boot knife between his teeth through the bandanna covering his face, then pushed himself to his feet and ran. He vaulted the fence, quickly, more easily than he thought he could, the man on the porch turning, snapping away the cigarette butt in his right hand, and almost as if in slow motion moving the right hand toward the pistol in his trouser band.

Frost neared the porch, starting to reach for the railing, seeing the man moving the pistol on line now.

Frost vaulted the railing, his feet flailing out, hammering against the chest of the man as the gun levelled on him. The man rocked back, Frost toppling to the porch floor, falling.

The guard was falling, the pistol hitting the floorboards of the porch, not discharging. Frost snatched the knife from his teeth as he pushed himself up and threw his body forward, toward the man. Frost's right hand hammered down, cutting into the subclavial artery, Frost's left hand covering the mouth to stifle any scream.

There was none, the man's eyelids fluttering open, then locking that way—dead.

Frost thumbed them closed, pulling out the knife,

wiping it clean of blood and putting it back in his teeth.

He rose to a crouch, listening for sounds that the little noise there had been had awakened someone in the house. He heard nothing.

Frost took up the man's pistol—a Colt Combat Commander with the Satin Nickel finish. He dumped the magazine, then worked the slide, jacking out the chambered round.

Awkwardly because of the still-wet, fingerless gloves he wore, Frost turned out the barrel busing, releasing and recoil spring plug, quickly fieldstripping the pistol and tossing the barrel and recoil spring into a nearby bush, then leaving the metal parts on the floor of the porch, the pistol useless now to anyone who would find it.

A smile crossed his lips—the guys in movies and on television always left loaded guns behind them, which could be used on them. But they never were. Frost sometimes wished he were in the movies—life would be safer.

He started toward the screen door of the little canal house, standing beside it, listening—there was still no sound.

He tried the door and it gave.

Sucking in his breath, he started inside.

He stopped, just inside the door, beside the frame, the door creaking as he tried closing it behind him, all the house in darkness.

He started across the front room, the darkness now a greyness, his eye accustomed to the poorer light. There was a noise, and Frost wheeled, dodging instinctively from the sound, the lights in the house flashing on, the brightness partially blinding him as a machete sliced through the air inches from his head.

"Shit," Frost stammered, hitting the floor and going into a roll as a bull of a man spun around, wielding the machete again like a samurai sword in a martial arts cata. Frost started to his feet, edging away from the flashing blade of the machete, suddenly feeling something behind him, starting to turn—but his arms were pinned at his sides.

The man with the machete grinned broadly and slowed his pace, starting toward Frost as Frost struggled against the arms holding him.

Frost tried the standard gambit, inhaling hard to expand his chest, then letting out the breath and dropping. As Frost inhaled, the man holding his arms at his sides just tightened his pressure.

Frost tried another standard ploy—he crashed his right heel down on the instep of the man behind him. There was a loud curse, unintelligible, but no easing of the pressure.

The man with the machete was starting his swing.

Frost edged his right hand back, finding the testicles of the man holding him, then grabbed them, twisting, yanking, gouging.

There was a scream, more animal than human, and the pressure around Frost's arms and chest eased, Frost ramming his left elbow back, into the solar plexus of the man behind him, then Frost dropped down into a crouch as the machete sliced through the air where only a split second earlier his head and neck had been.

Frost smashed his right elbow back, into the left kneecap of the man who'd held him, then rolled, the machete slicing down again.

Frost backstepped, across the room, the man with the machete coming, the big man who'd pinned his arms now unsteadily on his feet, lurching forward as well.

Frost started to reach for his pistol as the man who'd held him brandished a push button knife, the blade arcing out, clicking into locked position audibly.

"Ohh—come on guys," Frost rasped, but both men kept coming—toward him.

Frost pulled the High Power and lowered the safety, the man with the machete charging.

Frost shot him twice in the throat, the body lurching forward, carried by its own momentum, blood gushing from the mouth and nose, the eyes already dead and staring.

Frost sidestepped, the man with the push button knife making a pass at him.

Frost shot him in the head . . .

Police would be coming soon, having heard the shots or a neighbor reporting them. Frost glanced at his watch as he entered the first room—a vacant bedroom. Vacant except for two crates. Frost used the push button knife from the second guard to pry at the lid of one of the crates. The knife blade snapped as the box lid came up. Frost threw the rest of the knife away, pulling up the box lid now with his hands from its partial opening.

The contents identically matched those of the crate on the small plane he had hijacked out of Colombia—styrofoam peanut-shaped packing material, and buried under a mound of it several packages wrapped in Bogota newspapers—Frost imagined that even now Colombian authorities were pressing their search for whatever connection existed between someone in Bogota and someone in Havana who supplied explosives.

And under the layers of Bogota newspapers were innocuous-looking grey blocks, for all the world like professional quality modeling clay in appearance. But the smell, the consistency—it was plastique, explosives in sufficient quantity—Frost began unearthing more bricks in the crate—to kill thousands.

He left the other crate, assuming the contents identical. Systematically, he began inspecting the nap in the carpeting on the bedroom floor. Where the nap was bent, fine lines could be seen if he looked at the carpet from the right angle. Three other crates had been in the room at least, and were now gone.

Frost moved on to the second bedroom. He flicked on the light—the impressions on the carpet here were clearer—five crates, gone now.

"Eight," he muttered to himself. Enough plastique to—he didn't know what.

He started toward the front door, hearing in the distance now the wailing of a police siren, not knowing if it was coming to the house or not, but not caring to wait in order to find out.

Frost started across the living room, then through the screen door and onto the porch.

He heard the screech of tires from the front of the house, on the opposite side of the canal and started to run, across the yard, toward the fence, flipping it as the automatic weapons fire started behind him. "Not cops," he rasped as he went over the fence, landing clumsily on the sand and grass and starting past the hedgerow toward the water.

He looked behind him once, then dove into the water, a hail of bullets around him. He still had no idea where Oriana Vasquez had been, but he knew where she was now—with Miranda Ceballos and with three men, all of them with submachineguns.

The water above him was boiling with the impact of bullets as Frost swam—he hoped he could hold his breath long enough. . .

Chapter Twenty-seven

Frost locked the rental car and started across the parking lot, stuffing the black bandannas into the pockets of his sodden black jeans, his combat boots tied together by the laces and slung across his left shoulder, the Browning—wet—and his other gear in an olive drab G.I. Cargo pack he'd picked up at a war surplus Army-Navy store a while back.

He reached the elevator, looking around, behind him, expecting some of Oriana's men to have followed him. But although there was no sign of anyone yet, the one-eyed man knew it was just a matter of time.

He took the elevator, nervous as he always was since that time in France*, but the ride to his floor was uneventful.

He let himself into his room, the key in his left hand, the Metalifed High Power in his right hand.

The room was vacant, untouched. He closed the door, locked it, then moved a chair in front of it. None of the safety devices would stop anyone wanting to burst into the room, only slow them slightly and make for more noise.

Frost sat on the bed, cradling the telephone against

*See, They Call Me The Mercenary #, *Fourth Reich Death Squad* his right shoulder while he busied his hands stripping the water-soaked spare magazines for his pistol, depressing the little spring-loaded detent in the base plate, sliding the base plates out, then the spring and the follower for each, wiping them clean, taking the small black plastic bottle of Break-Free CLP and cleaning and lubricating.

The home number for Lew Wilson wasn't answering. Frost tried the office, waiting a long time on hold while a secretary checked Wilson's whereabouts.

Frost had the magazines back in shape, then began reloading them. As he finally began working on the magazine that had been in the pistol, fresh cartridges in all the others, the secretary came back on the line. "I think Mr. Wilson had an appointment this morning—but he should be in within an hour. Can I have him—"

"No—tell Lew I'll call him. This is Hank Frost. I won't be at my hotel. Don't forget to tell him I called—it's important," and Frost hung up.

He finished the last magazine, then set the KG-99 on the bed beside him, just in case, field-stripping the High Power, cleaning it, then reassembling it quickly. He left the grips until last, since the gun would work without them. He removed the black checkered Pachmayr rubber grips with the small Colt sight adjustment screw driver he'd picked up years ago from a Colt Woodsman box. He cleaned around the grip frame, then oiled heavily where the grips would be and replaced them. As always, the Metalife SS Chromium M finish his pal Ron Mahovsky had applied was perfect. Frost jacked a fresh magazine into the pistol and worked the slide, leaving the gun cocked and locked.

He glanced at his watch, deciding to risk a shower.

As he started across the room, he stripped, dropping the wet clothes on the floor.

In the bathroom, the High Power beside him on top of the flush tank, he shaved, then brushed and flossed his teeth—he might not be back in a hotel room for some time, he reasoned. Life would be busy once he got hold of Lew Wilson.

Frost rinsed his toothbrush and closed the box of dental floss, then moved the High Power closer to the shower, on top of a towel on the edge of the sink. He started the water, washing his hair, his body, then rinsing under straight cold water for a moment.

He killed the shower, then climbed out, drying his still-dripping body as he moved across the room.

He pulled a white shirt, black socks, black knit tie and underpants from his Safariland SWAT Bag, then started to dress, his white suit just cleaned and pressed, but losing its shape as he dumped the spare magazines for the High Power into the pockets. He slipped the Cobra Comvest across his shoulders, holstered the High Power and shrugged into the jacket of his suit. He stuffed the KG-99 and its spare magazines, all his spare ammo and his razor, toothbrush and dental floss into the G.I. Cargo Pack, then made sure he had his wallet, his money clip and his keys, then removed the chair from in front of the door. He worked the chain open, then the security lock, then opened the door, slowly, after first peering through the little spy hole in the door.

There was no one in the hall except a maid. Frost left the little sign on the knob turned to "Do Not Disturb," then started toward the elevators. He pressed all the buttons, waiting for the first one in whichever bank came first, up or down. It was an up elevator and he took it, riding the empty elevator to the top floor. It stopped on the way down, at his floor and his right hand slipped under his coat to the Cobra Comvest and the butt of the Metalifed Browning. A woman entered, pretty enough, wearing a short jacket that looked as though it were made out of a towel, apparently covering up a swimsuit.

Blonde, blue eyed, she smiled at Frost and Frost smiled back. "Lobby?" he asked.

"Yes," she nodded, and Frost pushed the button again, the door closing.

He watched the floors counting downward, then on impulse pushed the button for the second floor. "Forgot something," he smiled, slipping out as the doors opened.

He ran toward the staircase, starting down, his hand under his coat just in case.

He reached the lobby, opposite the elevator bank, seeing a half dozen men and Miranda Ceballos starting toward the elevator bank.

Frost slipped outside into the steamy morning, whistling low under his breath . . .

He took a taxi across the water and back into Miami proper, finding a restaurant and going in, ordering steak and eggs and hash browns, then leaving his Cargo Pack in the booth and threading his way to the public telephones past a few bleary-eyed morning patrons. He dialed Lew Wilson's office, got the same secretary, and she told him Lew still wasn't in. Frost told her, "I'll call back — tell him to stay away from my hotel." He hung up and returned to his breakfast.

F.M. music—the canned variety—was playing from a radio by the counter and Frost automatically checked his watch when the news came on, half-heartedly listening for possible press notices on his activities the previous night. There was mention of three dead men found in what was apparently a drug smugglers' warehouse by one of the canals, but nothing about explosives. "Managed news," Frost smiled, forking a piece of steak drenched in sunny-side up egg into his mouth.

He started a forkful of potatoes into his mouth, but stopped—". . . of the Cuban Community. The court injunction not given, the train carrying the toxic materials to a portside rendezvous with a contract freighter will be travelling by the same route as originally intended, the same route which leaders of the Cuban Community said was too close to the heavily Cuban populated area of—"

Frost set down the fork, listening. ". . . the toxic chemicals are not a danger to life or property. The Defense Department spokesmen further went on to say that it is not the desire of the Defense Department to place any citizen, regardless of national origin, in jeopardy. It is for this specific reason that the chemicals will be disposed of far out to sea—"

"Holy shit," Frost murmured, downing his coffee and tossing a ten dollar bill on the table.

He walked out of the restaurant, remembering a paper machine outside. He found change and picked up the daily, seeing a small article about the train carrying the chemicals at the bottom of the front page. He read, ". . . contend that these are not toxic chemicals, but instead nerve gas. Defense Department spokesmen deny this allegation vigorously. The next move is up to the Cuban Community, but it will apparently be after the fact as the train is scheduled to move along the perimeter of Miami on schedule today . . ."

Frost tossed the newspaper into a trash can, lighting a cigarette, walking now.

It was all coming together—for once in his life he felt like a detective. But he wished that he didn't. He stopped by a pay phone, tried Lew Wilson again and this time got him. "Lew—Hank."

"Was that you last night with—"

"Hey—no time for that. I know what they're doing with the explosives—I know it all, and there isn't any time at all. Send a car for me," and Frost gave him the intersection. The one-eyed man hung up the phone and lit another cigarette. After all the years, all the killing, there were some things he still had a difficult time conceiving of his fellow man as being capable of doing. This was one of those things. "Nerve gas," he murmured, inhaling hard on the cigarette.

Oriana and Miranda—Frost decided they were among the most elite class of people, those capable of the unthinkable.

Chapter Twenty-eight

"We had the whole line checked—and a lot of the workmen who checked it were Cubans."

Frost looked at the railroad executive and smiled. "Whose Cubans—ours or theirs?"

"What?"

"What he means," Wilson interrupted, "is did you run background checks on your people, to make sure none of them were pro-Castro—"

"Background checks on trackmen—you're nuts, that'd cost a—"

"Could cost a lot of lives," Frost snapped, turning away and staring out into the switchyard. Seeing his own reflection like a ghost in the glass, Frost asked, "You can't reroute it?"

"No—it's already on the—"

"You can't stop it?"

"Not without orders from the Department of Defense—"

"I got a call in—but nothing yet," Wilson interjected.

"Shit," Frost murmured.

"I don't—I don't have to listen—to listen to this!" the railroad executive stammered.

"Listen to the screams of the dying then," Frost

answered and walked out, waiting on the elevated platform above the winding steps leading down into the railyard. "You don't have to—" he snarled under his breath.

The door opened and closed behind him. It was Lew Wilson.

"Well?" Frost asked.

"If you're wrong, I hope you can get me a job somewhere—come on," and Wilson started down the steps, Frost slapping his old friend on the shoulder . . .

Wilson drove, Frost smoked. "Run it by me again," Wilson murmured.

"All right," Frost sighed, studying the streets through which they drove—too quickly for the traffic, but too slowly for what lay ahead. "All right. Oriana and Miranda. Miranda is one of these people who can turn sex on and off like a tap—right? Probably that female terrorist she was hanging around with down in Colombia—probably her lover too. I figure she was a Communist all along, even before her father died. One of these people born rich who feels they have to destroy wealth to apologize to the world because they have it. She realized who Oriana was and figured having something on her could prove useful in the future."

"Aww, come on—that's the part I don't buy."

"It's the part that explains the whole thing, Lew—think about it," Frost insisted. "Beautiful girl, kind of on the aloof side—probably a hard time making friends. Meets another Spanish-speaking girl who's rich, beautiful—they become friends. They have a lesbian affair and Miranda has something on Oriana for life. Oriana's no Communist—she has every reason in the world to hate them. They killed her mother, almost killed her, made her an exile. Right? What other explanation is there for the two of them working together?"

"A bunch, maybe—hell, I don't know."

"No—had to be," Frost went on. "Only thing Miranda could frame her with. No one would believe Oriana would be working with the Communists, have her father killed—but what could be more damning? A homosexual affair with a Communist? If that came out, it'd be death for her in almost every way. She's beautiful, desirable—never had any steady boyfriend, never married, no love affairs—nothing at all."

"Maybe she just isn't interested in—hell," and Wilson hammered his fist on the steering wheel.

"Then what else could Miranda have on her to get her to work with her? Where was Oriana last night? Why did she show up with Miranda Ceballos? How did they work so closely together—huh? Think about it. What'd Joe say?"

"He said he set you up sending you down there—Miranda had been suspect for the last six months, but you getting out of there cleared her completely."

"And I also knocked off her boyfriend who was the only thing blocking her from leadership in M-19."

"But you just said it yourself—boyfriend!"

"She's bisexual—asexual—I don't know. But she does it for personal gain, not anything else, damnit!"

"Aww, come on—"

"Look—I know when a woman is—"

"Faking it? You oughta bottle that then."

"No—I mean the way she responded to me was

more than it should have been—a lot more. Hell—I don't know how to explain it, but it was. And the other night clinched it—I didn't realize it until I was walking down that street and I called you."

"What?"

"When I went to talk to Oriana. She looked like she was getting ready to go out—and obviously she did."

"So?"

"All the times I was around her, there was always something peculiar about her, odd—and I finally figured what it was."

"What—she dropped her shawl again and people kept getting shot around her?"

"Stop tryin' to be funny. It was somethin' real. She never wore perfume."

"Probably a lotta dames don't—"

"Let me finish—until the other night. And it struck me as odd, and then I finally remembered where I'd smelled it before. When I was strung up in that tiger cage in that hut at M-19 headquarters and Miranda came for me. She'd changed clothes, washed her hair—was all clean. And that's where I smelled the perfume. The same one Oriana was wearing, the only one I ever knew her to wear."

"What—two women were wearing the same perfume, they—"

"What would you do if you knew a certain woman you liked loved a certain aftershave?"

"Well, I'd—"

"With a woman, it'd be more obvious. Oriana never wears perfume, Miranda does. So Oriana wears the same scent to please Miranda. Obviously it pleases Miranda—she wears it."

"You tryin' to say I just ordered up a bunch of helicopters, a SWAT Team and—shit! Just because of a perfume?"

"Lew," Frost almost shouted. "I'm no cop, I'm no lawyer—evidence isn't my bag at all. But I know it. And Miranda used Oriana to set up this deal with the explosives. Blow up the train, kill thousands of innocent people and discredit the United States Government, then stick the blame to Omega Seven. What kind of explosives are those?"

"C-4—like they used in Viet Nam."

"American," Frost said. "American explosives—and I betchya Oriana set up some of her own men so the explosives can be traced right back to them. Then she takes off, disappears, and defects to Cuba, saying how disenchanted she is with the U.S., with American lies—the whole propaganda shot. And Miranda? She's not only head of M-19, she's on Castro's birthday list from now on."

"We don't even know that's nerve gas—could just be toxic chemicals, like the Defense Department says it is. That wouldn't cause the destruction that—"

"Well—we're gonna find out," Frost said soberly.

"Yeah—such a deal. You find out, I lose my job."

Frost laughed, saying, "Pessimist."

Chapter Twenty-nine

"Just on the off chance you guys are right," the FBI agent said, "what the hell good would it do to stop the train? Just make it a sitting duck. We gotta move it through and out."

Frost nodded. "Agreed—yeah." He lit a cigarette, inhaling deeply.

"Then what do we do—just if we might be right?" Wilson asked.

"We board the train—some of your men, some of mine and we give it a lookover. He can't come," the FBI agent said, gesturing at Frost.

Frost smiled, saying, "What the hell you mean—'he can't come'?"

"You're a civilian—a mercenary—what the hell you think I mean?"

"You know Mike O'Hara?"

"Yeah," the agent answered noncommittally.

"Then you get your ass onto the phone with him right now—and see if I can't come," Frost answered. "And damn quick—every minute we waste talkin' is another minute closer to a bomb going off on that train."

"Do it," Wilson told the FBI man.

The agent stalked off, between two waiting helicopters and toward a grey F.O.U.O.* Ford.

*F.O.U.O.—"For Official Use Only"

Frost stubbed out his cigarette on a low brick wall beside him, listening to Wilson saying, "Take it easy Hank—the guy's just tryin' to do his job. If you're right and you're not there, you'll be just as right."

"I just got a feeling Lew—that I gotta be there. I'm not tryin' to make you a hard time with the Feds—I know you work with 'em."

"Then don't forget to tell everybody you were home in bed last night," Wilson laughed.

"A good five boxes worth of explosives were missing out of that house, Lew," Frost told him.

"What house—how would you know about it?" Wilson smiled.

"Let's say I heard a rumor—huh?"

Wilson shook his head, saying, "If you'd racked up any more little side trips, hell—there would've been a crime wave last night."

"What side trips?" Frost laughed.

The FBI man was coming back, between the two helicopters. He stopped, lighting a filter-tipped cigarette, then said, "You're the same Frost that saved the life of the President of the United States that time—aren't you?"*

"Yeah—that's me," Frost grinned.

"O'Hara says if I don't figure out a way of taking you along, he'll do something about it."

"Was he any more specific?"

"Shut up—you're coming," the FBI agent snapped.

Frost felt that if he could have seen his own face in a mirror, he would have looked like the cat who swallowed the canary. He just hoped he didn't wind

*See, They Call Me The Mercenary #8, *Assassin's Express*

up with nothing more than a mouth full of feathers . . .

The helicopter touched down and Frost released the restraint harness on the seat and jumped out, the wind whipping at his hair, his half-mast neck tie. In the distance along the right of way, Frost could see the diesel engine and the train it pulled, slowing already as Wilson joined him now. Frost started away from the chopper, the FBI agent—Roger Hemingway—coming around from the other side of the helicopter.

"That train technically isn't supposed to stop," the FBI agent shouted, "so it's gonna slow and we're getting aboard. You better be right, Wilson—cause Frost there isn't the one with his job on the line."

Wilson said nothing, just starting toward the tracks, Frost running beside him, Hemingway falling into step, bringing up the rear.

Nothing distinguished the train on the outside as being anything other than ordinary—except for the two passenger cars, and Frost had learned these were loaded with military personnel—a detachment of troops the Army had provided, since the "hazardous chemicals" were theirs to begin with.

The train was slowing more now and Hemingway shouted, "All right—let's go," Hemingway jumping for one of the troop cars, Frost and Wilson jumping for the rear door of the same car.

Enlisted men with M-16s waited for them.

"I'm Lew Wilson—special agent with the Florida Department of Law Enforcement," Wilson told the ranking man. The man nodded, saying nothing.

As Wilson and Frost started through into the car, the nearest trooper opened the door for them. Frost followed Wilson inside, seeing Hemingway at the far end of the car, conferring with a fatigue-clad First Lieutenant. Between Hemingway and where Frost stood swaying with the motion of the train were twenty men, like the troopers who had met them at the rear door of the car, armed with M-16s, their faces ranging from bored to nervous.

Wilson started down the aisle, Frost behind him.

When they reached Hemingway, the First Lieutenant he was speaking with turned and nodded. "Gentlemen—I understand there's some sort of problem with our train—you think there's some sort of bomb."

"Gotta be," Frost told the officer. "Ton of explosives missing that were smuggled in by pro-Castro terrorists from Colombia—the cards are right for this to be the target."

"You're Captain Frost, I take it," the young officer smiled.

"That's right, Lieutenant."

"Well—let's check it out." The younger man started past Frost down the length of the passenger car, stopping to talk with a Sergeant First Class. They conferred for a moment, the Sergeant saluting and the Lieutenant returning it, then starting back toward Frost, Wilson and Hemingway.

"I'll accompany you gentlemen—and we'll check this out. My men have already searched both of the troop cars—nothing. If there's a bomb, it's ahead of us or in the caboose behind us. But frankly—it's impossible. This train has been so heavily guarded ever since it was assembled, no one could have planted a stray toothpick let alone plastique or something like that," the Lieutenant insisted.

"How do we get to the freight cars?" Frost asked.

"Not like in the movies—just walk on through—these are specially constructed with side access doors for inspections."

Frost nodded, following the young Lieutenant through onto the platform between the cars formed by the front of the passenger car and the rear of the special freight car. The Lieutenant produced a set of keys, gave what sounded like a password but might have been an ordinary greeting to the two enlisted men by the freight car side door, then worked the key on the padlock. He opened the door, starting inside, a flashlight in his left hand.

Hemingway had one as well, Frost and Wilson following behind him.

The cones of yellow light flashed across the nearly dark freight car, slats in the walls of the car wide apart enough that slivers of sunlight filtered in, but the isolated lines of light only serving to intensify the overall darkness.

Frost reached across and took Hemingway's light without asking, flashing it on the cannisters stored in the freight car. "It is nerve gas," he murmured.

The Lieutenant's light shot into Frost's face. "Yes—but what you see here, gentlemen, goes no further. If we'd admitted this was gas there would have been a needless panic."

"Let's look for the bomb," Frost told him—he shone the light around the freight car. "Then we can see how needless it is to panic."

As Frost began to search the car, he realized the search was probably futile. If a bomb had gotten this far, it could have been disguised as one of the cannisters of gas itself. And he realized that likely none of the enlisted men aboard the train knew what they guarded. "Hell," Frost rasped . . .

An hour's searching in both cars proved useless. As they left the second car, their way barred ahead of them now by a second diesel engine and the primary diesel, the Lieutenant smiled broadly, saying, "I could have predicted this, gentlemen. No bomb."

"No job," Wilson muttered, looking away.

The FBI man—Hemingway—smiled smugly. "Looks like you were wrong, Frost."

"Captain Frost," the Lieutenant began, his voice conciliatory sounding to the one-eyed man. "You've got to appreciate the care we took with this entire operation. Not only was the train isolated by a security cordon, but every inch of track was inspected along the way. I'll give you an example," and he pointed up along the length of the train past the two diesel engines. "About ten miles ahead of us—maybe fifteen—there's a bridge. Some vandals had apparently damaged it and when the damage was discovered, a special crew was put on to repair the bridge. Worked on it all last night."

"We've gotta stop the train," Frost told the young Lieutenant.

"For God's sake, why? We didn't find any—"

"Don't be a dead fool—that bridge. Last night the terrorists who planned this thing moved their explosives. Last night, one of the ring leaders of the group was missing all night. There's a Communist M-19 terrorist working with them and I saw her last night with the other woman."

"Women—terrorists? What could a couple of

women do—"

Frost took a step closer to the young officer, his face now inches from the man's face. "A woman can detonate a bomb just as easily as a man, kid—and that bridge is one super hunk of plastique just waiting to go."

Hemingway started to say something. Wilson told him, "Just shut up, Roger—will ya?"

Chapter Thirty

The cocky expression was gone from the Lieutenant's face—one of unease, even fear replacing it. "I can't contact the engine," the younger man said.

"What do you mean?" Hemingway asked.

"I have tried contacting him—the engineer. There were two of my men up there with him. There's no answer. Probably something with the radio—"

"Now listen," Frost told him, looking at the young army officer, then looking at Hemingway as well.

"Could be all sorts of rational explanations why the engine isn't responding. Bad radio, freak interference—all sorts of things. Or could it be one of your men, or the engineer was working for the Castro people. Either way, we've either got nobody running the train or we've got a terrorist up there or at the least we have no way to stop this sucker. And we hit that bridge and—"

"Look—that's—"

There was a gunshot, then a long burst of automatic weapons fire and the Lieutenant keeled over forward into Frost's arms, the two enlisted men by the door into the freight car returning fire. Frost caught the Lieutenant, keeping him from falling off the platform, ducking as more gunfire streamed toward them. One of the enlisted men was shot in the jaw and went down, the younger of the two wounded in the thigh.

"The road down there!" Wilson shouted, pulling his gun.

Frost looked behind him, resting the Lieutenant's head against his leg, in the direction Wilson was looking. A road—Frost thought it would inevitably be named Frontage Road or something similiar—paralleled the railroad tracks, and along the road, passing the train, ran three automobiles, men with gas-masks covering their faces and automatic weapons in their hands leaning from the open car windows, firing.

Hemingway already had his revolver out, returning fire down into the road, as was the one enlisted man with the leg wound.

Frost glanced at the Lieutenant. The man—boy—was dead.

"Hemingway—roust that Sergeant back in the first troop car. We're gonna need help."

Hemingway nodded, starting back toward the door of the freight car.

Wilson fired a rapid semi-automatic burst from his Beretta 92SB, then pulled back, the steel of the freight car frame ripping under the impact of an automatic weapons burst. "World War III," Wilson shouted.

"Naw—I fought that one the other day," Frost shouted, his Metalifed High Power out, the hammer back. "We gotta get to that engine."

"I know—gimme a minute here," and Frost started firing the Browning down toward the pursuit cars as Wilson turned to his radio. "Wilson to strike force—come in. Wilson to strike force—come in."

Static, then a crackling voice came over the two way radio. "Strike Force—we hear gunfire, Wilson—confirm."

"You're hearin' right—got three cars, all heavily armed. Taking a lot of gunfire, apparently the engine is under control of the terrorists or without an engineer completely. Got one dead infantry First Lieutenant, a severely wounded Corporal with a bullet in his face, and another enlisted man with a leg wound. Need medics, need your choppers to get these damned cars off our tails. One of their stray slugs hits one of these gas cannisters—" Wilson shut off.

"Gas? Say again!"

"Gas—nerve gas—Frost recognized it. Now hurry up with that air support. Frost and I are going for the engine."

"Roger on that, out."

"Wilson out," and Wilson stuffed the radio set back into the pocket of his suit.

Already a fusillade of gunfire was coming from the train cars, aimed at the cars below, but still heavy automatic weapons fire poured up at them.

"You ready?" Wilson asked.

"Over the top, I guess," Frost answered. Then the one-eyed man looked at the young enlisted man with the leg wound. "You hold the fort here?"

"Nobody's gettin' past me, sir."

Frost smiled, saying, "Way to go son," then started after Wilson toward the far side of the platform separating the lead freight car from the second engine.

There was a narrow railing—apparently for service use—running the length of the engine, and Wilson stepped out off the platform and onto it. "At least we're out of their sights," Wilson shouted back, Frost following him. Then Wilson tucked down, a burst of automatic weapons fire coming at Frost and Wilson from the lead engine.

"Aww shit," Frost snarled. "They got somebody up there waiting for us!"

Wilson pulled back, beside Frost behind the shelter of the nose of the second diesel.

"Look!" Frost shouted, gesturing skyward, a helicopter starting diagonally toward them. "Looks like our—" The words died in his throat. The helicopter, he realized, had come from the wrong direction. "Get down, Lew!"

Submachinegun fire raked the platform between the box car and the diesel, Frost and Wilson tucking down, the young wounded trooper pulling back, holding his fire as bullets hammered around him, ricocheting, pinging against the metal surfaces.

"Keep down son—no sense getting killed," Frost ordered the boy.

On his left arm, slung there across his back, Frost had the KG-99. He slid it forward, holstering the High Power now.

He handed the KG-99 to Wilson for a moment. "Lew—I'm goin' up front—with this. Across the top of the engine—only way. Too much direct fire on that little catwalk. Take an M-16 and—"

"I know—improvise," Wilson smiled.

The one-eyed man laughed, snatching up an M-16 and handing it to Wilson. Then Frost slung the KG-99 cross body from his left shoulder, suspended under his right arm. He started forward, clambering up at the edge of the catwalk, gunfire roaring down on him, the headlight of the diesel shattering in gunfire from above.

Frost leaned against the side of the catwalk, working the bolt on the KG-99, then starting up, onto the top of the diesel engine itself. A broad expanse of glass was under him—the windshield. He braced his left foot against the windshield wiper, Wilson reaching up with his left hand, bracing Frost's foot as well. More submachinegun fire as the helicopter overhead made

210

another pass. The glass shattered under him, around him, Frost falling through the disintegrated windshield, to the floor of the second locomotive cab.

His head ached, banged against a seat back, his back aching from the bizarre angle at which he'd fallen. He could hear Wilson shouting over the roar of gunfire, the pinging of metal. "Hank! Hank!"

"All right!" Frost shouted back. "All right!" The one-eyed man pushed himself to his feet, his back aching still, shards of glass falling from his clothes as he stood.

The KG-99 in an assault position, he started forward, along the length of the locomotive interior, stopping near the air intake vents for the engine. "Hell," he rasped, his way blocked except for a narrow causeway to the side of the engines. There was clear passage to the rear of the engine, and then to the rear of the lead engine, but if the subgunner in the lead engine started shooting, once Frost was in the passage, there would be nowhere to go, no place to hide—he'd be dead, a sitting duck.

Frost looked at the KG-99 in his hands, grasping it by the pistol grip with his right and the front pistol grip in his left. He started down the passageway, slowly, eyeing the front diesel. There was more gunfire from behind and above him, bullets zinging off the metal bodywork of the train, glass shattering, heavier sounds of gunfire where Wilson and the wounded young soldier would be returning fire. "Where's the damned air support?" Frost muttered, still moving toward the rear of the diesel.

He was six feet from the rear access door now, his fists tight on the gun in his hands, his eye locked on the rear door of the forward engine, the throbbing of the diesel ahead of him already intense.

The rear door of the forward diesel swung open. Frost could see it, almost in freeze frame, as a man from the front compartment levelled a submachinegun toward the glass of the rear diesel's access door. The glass shattered as Frost dove to the floor of the passageway, the glass around him on both sides of the passage walls shattering under the impact of the metal case bullets hammering along the passage.

The noise, the whining of ricochets—it was maddening. Frost covered his face with his left arm as glass from the windows and the gauge covers shattered around him, over him.

The submachinegun fire kept up, up, unceasing. The man was burning out the entire magazine, Frost realized. And that would give him one chance, maybe three seconds at the outside, he knew.

The subgun fire stopped and Frost pushed up to his feet, pumping the trigger of the KG-99, again and again as he ran the length of the passageway, reaching the rear door, dimpled with slug impacts, the glass shot out and gone, wind from the diesel's slipstream tearing at his face and his hair.

He rammed the KG-99 through the open window and kept firing, the subgunner standing there, ramming his fresh magazine home into the Uzi in his hands, less than two yards from Frost.

Frost kept pumping the trigger of the semi-automatic KG-99, the body of the subgunner starting to twist, to turn, to spin, the subgun falling from his hands, the body falling, landing perilously close to the edge of the platform behind the lead diesel.

Frost shoved open the door of the second diesel, the door sticking against the shards of broken glass under the seal. He threw his weight against it, then pushed again, sliding through. The wind of the slipstream whipped his tie against his face now. Frost shoved the end of the tie inside his shirt, stepping forward toward the dead subgunner.

But he wasn't dead. The man opened his eyes, looking up at Frost, almost pleadingly from where he hung half over the edge of the platform.

The one-eyed man took a half step back, kicking the subgunner in the face and rolling the body off the engine platform. There was a scream, as blood sprayed up across Frost's white suit as the body was sucked under the wheels of the train and chopped to pieces.

Frost changed sticks in the KG-99, two spares stuck in his belt on each side under his coat.

He worked the bolt, chambering a fresh round, giving him thirty-six.

He started forward into the identical tunnel in the lead diesel, wondering if another subgunner was waiting for him, his palms sweating, his hands tight on the KG-99.

He stopped at the edge of the engineer's compartment.

No subgunner waited for him. There were two bodies, throats slit, one an Army private, the second a Corporal. The man Frost had shot had been dressed as an engineer.

Frost eyed the myriad gauges of the instrument panel—they were shattered, the control arms broken off. If the train could be stopped, Frost didn't know how.

And ahead of him now, around a far bend in the right of way, he could see the bridge.

Mentally, Frost ran the options. He shook his head,

not liking the odds on the only one that made sense.

Frost leaned out the engineer's window, the gunfire still overhead, but more of it now. More helicopters were in the air—the air support! Frost shouted back along the length of the two engines. "Lew! Lew!"

Wilson peered around the corner of the nose of the rear engine. "You all right?"

"Yeah—get into that second engine, figure out how to start her up—in forward!"

"What?"

"Only chance," Frost shouted. "I'm gonna disconnect this engine— can't stop it. You get the other one going—soon as I disconnect the two engines, give her the juice!"

"That could derail us!"

"That bridge is about five minutes away—no choice!" Frost shouted.

Wilson seemed to Frost to hesitate for an instant, then shouted, "You'll get killed trying to uncouple these—if I get the—"

"Hell with it—I'll be all right!"

Frost threw open the engineer's door, debating whether to leave the KG-99 behind. But it was a friend now, after the gun battle. He slung it across his body, letting the gun ease behind his back, then started out onto the catwalk, along the side of the racing engine.

The gun battle overhead was a dogfight now, between the enemy chopper and the two helicopters of the strike team. Hearing gunfire from the road on the opposite side now, he could tell the cars were still there as well. It was a miracle that as yet a stray bullet hadn't impacted against one of the nerve gas cannisters. Ahead he could see the right of way bending. The bridge would be perhaps three minutes ahead now. He moved faster along the catwalk, reaching the edge of the platform. He had chosen the outside route because it would be faster—there were safety chains connecting the engines on each side, and from the platform it would have been necessary to climb out to get the one nearest the catwalk.

Frost leaned down now, releasing the nearest chain, then jumped toward the platform. He landed hard, almost twisting his ankle, but pushed himself to his feet. He reached out, disconnecting the opposite safety chain. Then Frost looked down under the connecting platform, the rails racing below him seemingly, the train almost appearing to be standing still. The coupling for the brakes—if he started braking the remaining cars, then Wilson's engine could get the leverage needed to push them back.

Frost edged closer to the rails, seeing the spots of blood on his white suit, remembering the death of the submachinegun-armed terrorist.

Frost's stomach churned as he reached out with his right hand to the coupling. He knew little about trains—if he released the coupling, it would cut the brake line for the air brakes and start to stop the rest of the train, then the fresh power surge of the second diesel—would it? He didn't know. He had the brake coupling in his hand now, starting to twist.

It wouldn't budge.

He leaned further forward, trying with both hands. It was greasy, but started to move, he thought. He summoned all his strength, inhaled and twisted the mechanism with both hands, feeling the pain in his fingers from the strain as the coupling moved free.

The brake line flexed away, whipping at Frost's hands.

Frost pushed himself up, the two engines, starting to split already. The one-eyed man jumped, his hands reaching for the platform rail of the second engine as the first engine pulled away under his feet.

His grip started to loosen, Frost throwing his weight forward, his body crashing down on the platform of the second engine.

He started to his feet, but the engine lurched under him and he fell back, grappling for the handrailing, the left hand grip slipping. He lurched forward again, crashing down on the platform.

The train was moving—in reverse, away from the bridge.

Frost turned around, staring ahead of him now as the first engine hit the bridge.

It moved out easily enough, toward the center of the trestle, then there was a roar, a shockwave hammering at his body, a flash of light, blinding bright, debris crashing toward him. Frost started to turn away, something hitting him, then only darkness . . .

Chapter Thirty-one

"I don't want you doing this, Hank—you're supposed to be in the hospital."

"You know—you missed your calling in Law Enforcement—should have been a railroad engineer."

"Look—I just lucked out and flipped the right combination of switches. I could have just as easily gotten us in reverse and pushed the lead engine and dragged us all onto the bridge."

"But you didn't," Frost told him.

"I mean it about you—that chunk of bridge or whatever almost peeled your scalp off."

Frost touched his left hand gingerly to the bandage on the side of his head. "But it didn't," he said brightly. "Besides—if this plane is supposed to pick them up, you couldn't pay me to miss it."

"It's only a rumor—a tip."

"Yeah—but there are a lot of people in the anti-Castro movement who'd love to tip the cops on Oriana now, aren't there."

Wilson shrugged. "Yeah—now that we briefed them on what almost happened. You know," Wilson said, his voice lowering. "If that ahh—that engine—if it had carried us onto that bridge, we would have been looking at maybe ten thousand deaths, not to mention the people on the train. At least. Maybe twenty thousand."

"What are you gonna do when this is all over," Frost asked his friend.

"Go sailing for a while—lose the cobwebs. How about you?"

"Few days—just about the time I can get rid of this bandage, Bess'll be back stateside—meeting me. She's got some kind of screwy assignment here for that news bureau she works for. We're gonna kind of use it like a working vacation."

"Well—take the vacation part of it," Wilson laughed. "You need it."

"Tell me about it," Frost smiled.

The car stopped, gravel crunching under the tires as the car rocked once on its brakes.

"Now what?"

"We wait—out there," Wilson answered, gesturing into the darkness.

Frost climbed out of the car, a little unsteady yet after two days in the hospital, his head aching—but he wouldn't tell Wilson that. The chance to nail Oriana Vasquez and Miranda Ceballos on their way out of the country to Cuba was too much to pass up.

He zipped the windbreaker he wore, cold in the darkness.

His only armament was the Metalifed High Power, and the Gerber knife. He was intent on leaving the shooting war part—if there were one—to Wilson and his men, Wilson pulling strings enough to get Frost along for the bust.

As they started into the palms to cross toward the field where the pickup was to take place, Frost wondered what he would say, if the chance presented itself, to Oriana, or especially to Miranda Ceballos. He dismissed the idea—there was nothing he could say that would show his contempt for them. Their sexual practices were their own business—once, years ago, Frost had stopped three guys who had been beating a homosexual man to death behind a garage up in Chicago. The reason the three men had given the police was that they didn't like homosexuals. Frost couldn't deal with reasoning like that—a person had a right to choose his own life. What disgusted Frost about Miranda and Oriana was something else—that Oriana had betrayed her father, causing his death, betrayed Omega Seven, brave men and women fighting against the Communist dictator who had usurped their homeland. And Miranda—scheming, conniving, brutal, cold—for betraying everyone for her own ends.

He swallowed hard, against the pain in his head, as he sat behind a clump of brush, waiting. He couldn't even smoke . . .

The line of dawn on the horizon was grey, with pink at its edges when Frost first heard the muted rumbling of the aircraft engine. And there was another engine sound, a car pulling up out of the pitch darkness at the far side of the field, lights off.

The car stopped, the headlights blinked once, then once again, then the dome light came on for an instant, someone getting out, and in the back seat, Frost imagined he saw two women. The light went out.

Frost watched the figure of a man walking around the field, setting out railroad flares, igniting them to form a crude, cross-shaped marker.

The small plane circled overhead, the light slightly brighter now and its outline barely visible.

The sound of the aircraft engine changed as the man lit the last of the flares, the circling of the plane ceasing, the engine noise dying.

"Relax—just coming in for landing."

"I know," Frost whispered to Wilson.

Frost could see the running lights, hear the sudden change in the engine noise as the pilot would be throttling back. It almost sounded as though the prop stalled once, but then the noise became more even again, the plane starting down, the tips of the wings catching the edge of light on the horizon.

The plane touched down, taxied and turned around, some of the flares burnt out already.

The dome light came on in the car, then a trunk light in the back. There was only one man, a suitcase in each hand, walking toward the plane, the same man who had lit the flares.

Frost recognized the bulk—it was Alberto, one of Oriana's father's guards. Frost had never suspected him.

The man left the suitcases beside the plane, the pilot out now, starting to stow them in the fuselage.

He walked back toward the car, opening the rear door, helping one, then a second figure from the car. Both were slender, obviously women by the shapes of their silhouettes in the darkness. Frost could tell that one wore a dress or skirt by the outline of the body.

The two women, Alberto on their far side, started toward the plane.

"Now," Wilson whispered into a small radio set.

Then Wilson stepped out of the brush, a flashlight held high in his left hand, above his head, the beam aimed toward the two women and the man, the Beretta in his right fist. "Police officers! Freeze—you are totally surrounded, give up!"

More than a dozen flashlights came on, trained on the two women and the man—Alberto's fists balling but empty of the twin Smith revolvers he habitually carried, Miranda, a gun in the waistband of her jeans, her hands at her sides, and Oriana, her shoulders huddled under a sweater worn across them, looking shaky in the high-heeled shoes she wore.

"Hands in the air," Wilson shouted.

Alberto looked at Miranda—Miranda nodded, and he raised his hands. Oriana raised her hands as well, the sweater dropping from her shoulders, her shoulders bare.

Miranda never moved. "Come ahead," she called out, squinting against the lights trained on her.

Frost stood up, walking beside Wilson—he could see five men at least with guns trained on the pilot who stood—frozen—beside the small aircraft.

A searchlight came on—Frost didn't even know Wilson had had one brought along, but the searchlight now completely blanketed the field in a cone around the two women and Alberto, the darkness through which Frost walked that much darker.

"I have a Cuban diplomatic passport," Miranda advised before they even reached her. "You cannot arrest me."

"We can sure as hell give it a good try," Wilson answered.

She looked nervously—the first time Frost could

have ever described her that way—at Alberto. He reached for his guns. "Look out," Frost shouted, going for his own pistol.

Alberto had both pistols, firing as more than a dozen guns returned shots, Alberto crumpling to the ground.

"Hold it!" It was Miranda. Frost looked at her, at her eyes—the nervous look of a second earlier was replaced by one of confidence, almost daring. In her right hand was her pistol—the little H-K automatic she had carried in Colombia. Her left arm was around Oriana's throat, pulling Oriana back at a bizarre angle, the muzzle of the pistol beside Oriana's head. "I will kill her!"

"Don't shoot," Wilson snapped.

"This one's all right—I think he'll make it," one of Wilson's men called out, crouched beside Alberto.

"He was always tough," Frost noted.

"You can't get—"

"I can do," she snapped, cutting off Wilson, "whatever I wish. Will you see me kill Miss Vasquez?"

Wilson didn't answer.

Frost raised the High Power, aiming it at Miranda's head. Frost, in the darkness, said, "I will Miranda—I'll kill you. And if you kill her, no big deal. What jury's gonna put me away for killing mass murderers and Communists."

"Hank! Damnit!"

"Stay out of it Lew," Frost snapped, edging away from his friend, into the spot light, the muzzle of his pistol less than three yards from Miranda's head. "I can't miss at this range even if I try, kid," Frost told her.

"Murder—you wouldn't—"

"Bullshit, lady," Frost sang out. "Try me! Put down the gun and step away, or there's Miranda Ceballos' brain all over the ground! What'll it be?"

"Hank!"

"Be cool, Lew," Frost told him. Then to Miranda, "Well—Miranda!"

He thought maybe it was something she saw in his face. She put the gun down, dropped it to the ground and stepped back.

"That's a real shame," Frost told her, putting down his gun, lighting a cigarette. "I was really hopin' I'd have the chance to blow you away—bitch."

Frost walked into the darkness. He was getting soft, he decided—he almost felt sorry for Oriana.

THE SURVIVALIST SERIES
by Jerry Ahern

THE SURVIVALIST #1: TOTAL WAR (768, $2.25)
The first in the shocking series that follows the unrelenting search for
ex-CIA covert operations officer John Thomas Rourke to locate his
missing family—after the button is pressed, the missiles launched and
the multimegaton bombs unleashed . . .

THE SURVIVALIST #2:
THE NIGHTMARE BEGINS (810, $2.50)
After WW III, the United States is just a memory. But ex-CIA covert
operations officer Rourke hasn't forgotten his family. While hiding
from the Soviet occupation forces, he adheres to his search!

THE SURVIVALIST #3: THE QUEST (851, $2.50)
Not even a deadly game of intrigue within the Soviet High Command,
the formation of the American "resistance" and a highly placed
traitor in the new U.S. government can deter Rourke from continuing
his desperate search for his family.

THE SURVIVALIST #4: THE DOOMSAYER (893, $2.50)
The most massive earthquake in history is only hours away, and
Communist-Cuban troops, Soviet-Cuban rivalry, and a traitor in the
inner circle of U.S.II block Rourke's path. But he must go on—he is
THE SURVIVALIST.

*Available wherever paperbacks are sold, or order direct from the
Publisher. Send cover price plus 50¢ per copy for mailing and han-
dling to Zebra Books, 475 Park Avenue South, New York, N.Y. 10016.
DO NOT SEND CASH.*